PUFFIN BOOKS

SEARCH FOR THE GOLDEN ACORN

Join Abby and Charlie as they travel backwards and forwards in time in their quest for the Golden Acorn, the key to their safe return home.

At the same time, you can find out about the National Trust and the houses and places it owns.

Search for the Golden Acorn is a story, a game, an information book and a challenge; solve all the puzzles that Abby and Charlie face, work out where the Golden Acorn is, and you could be among the lucky prizewinners.

SEARCH FOR THE GOLDEN ACORN

Michael Johnstone

Illustrated by Harry Venning

PUFFIN BOOKS
in association with the
NATIONAL TRUST

PUFFIN BOOKS

Published by the Penguin Group
Penguin Books Ltd, 27 Wrights Lane, London W8 5TZ, England
Penguin Books USA Inc., 375 Hudson Street, New York, New York 10014, USA
Penguin Books Australia Ltd, Ringwood, Victoria, Australia
Penguin Books Canada Ltd, 10 Alcorn Avenue, Toronto, Ontario, Canada M4V 3B2
Penguin Books (NZ) Ltd, 182 - 190 Wairau Road, Auckland, 10, New Zealand

Penguin Books Ltd, Registered Offices: Harmondsworth, Middlesex, England

First published in Puffin Books 1995
3 5 7 9 10 8 6 4 2

Copyright © Complete Editions 1995
All rights reserved

Design and typesetting by Michael Mepham, Frome, Somerset
Printed in England by Clays Ltd, St Ives plc

INTRODUCTION

Search for the Golden Acorn takes you on an unforgettable journey from Roman times right up to today. During your trip you will visit fifty National Trust properties, and at each one you will find a puzzle to solve to help you find where the Golden Acorn is hidden.

Begin by reading the story of how Abby and Charlie came to be lost in time, and how they found out that the key to their safe return to the present is a Golden Acorn that lies hidden in one of the National Trust properties. If you can find out where the Acorn is, you could receive a prize.

You have to solve fifty puzzles correctly. Each of them has three possible answers set out like this one, for the puzzle at Lacock Abbey:

If you choose	Letter	Number	Go to
1	W	6	*Anglesey Abbey (p76)*
2	C	5	*Knole (p86)*
3	O	4	*Alderley Edge (p44)*

If you think that 1 is the correct answer, turn to page vii, and write W and 6 in the spaces alongside Lacock Abbey. Then go to Anglesey Abbey and try to solve the puzzle there. If you think 2 is the answer, mark C and 5 in the spaces and go to Knole to solve the puzzle there. And so on. The puzzles take you backwards and forwards in time, to places all over England and Wales and Northern Ireland. The first puzzle is set at Charlecote Park and eventually you should find yourself back there.

If you find yourself in the same place twice (apart from Charlecote) then you will know you have made a mistake, so go back and try again!

At the end of your quest, the fifty letters will spell out a message that will help you find the Acorn. The more answers you get wrong, the more difficult it will be to read the message. You could remain lost in time for ever and ever.

Good luck!

THE COMPETITION

Enter the letter and number shown alongside the answer you chose here, next to the correct National Trust property. By the time you complete the page, you are well on the way to finding out where the Golden Acorn is hidden. (Extra clue: not everyone can spell as well as you!)

	Letter	Number		Letter	Number
A La Ronde			Colby Estate		
Aberglaslyn			Coniston Valley		
Alderley Edge			Coniston Water		
Allen Banks			Corfe Castle		
Anglesey Abbey			Cragside		
Argory			Danbury		
Arlington Court			Eaves & Waterslack Woods		
Ashdown Park					
Baddesley Clinton			Erddig		
Bateman's	B	8	Florence Court		
Beningbrough Hall	N	8	Frensham Common		
Black Down			Giant's Causeway		
Blackwater Estuary			Grasmere		
Boscastle Harbour			Greys Court		
Bradenham			Hadrian's Wall		
Brecon Beacons	N	3	Hughenden Manor		
Brownsea Island			Knole		
Buckland Abbey			Lacock Abbey	O	4
Calke Abbey			Lyme Park	R	3
Castle Ward			Oxburgh Hall		
Charlecote Park	I	5	Plas Newydd		
Chartwell			Runnymede		
Chedworth Villa	Q	7	St Michael's Mount		
Cherryburn			Stephenson's B'place		
Cliveden			Sutton House		
Clumber Park					

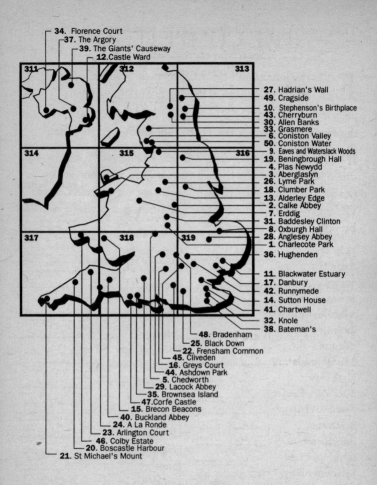

34. Florence Court
37. The Argory
39. The Giants' Causeway
12. Castle Ward

311
312
313

27. Hadrian's Wall
49. Cragside
10. Stephenson's Birthplace
43. Cherryburn
30. Allen Banks
33. Grasmere
6. Coniston Valley
50. Coniston Water
9. Eaves and Waterslack Woods
19. Beningbrough Hall
4. Plas Newydd
3. Aberglaslyn
26. Lyme Park
18. Clumber Park
13. Alderley Edge
2. Calke Abbey
7. Erddig
31. Baddesley Clinton
8. Oxburgh Hall
28. Anglesey Abbey
1. Charlecote Park
36. Hughenden

314
315
316

11. Blackwater Estuary
17. Danbury
42. Runnymede
14. Sutton House
41. Chartwell
32. Knole
38. Bateman's

317
318
319

48. Bradenham
25. Black Down
22. Frensham Common
45. Cliveden
16. Greys Court
44. Ashdown Park
5. Chedworth
29. Lacock Abbey
35. Brownsea Island
47. Corfe Castle
15. Brecon Beacons
40. Buckland Abbey
24. A La Ronde
23. Arlington Court
46. Colby Estate
20. Boscastle Harbour
21. St Michael's Mount

When you have worked out the message, the map reference and magic words (the clue that gives you these words is in the story), and know where the Golden Acorn is, write the answers in the space opposite and fill in your name, address, telephone number and age.

Then carefully tear out this page and send it to:

Search for the Golden Acorn
Puffin Books,
27 Wrights Lane,
London W8 5TZ

to arrive no later than 31st December 1995.

If your answers are correct, they will be entered in a draw on 5th January 1996. The first 50 winners and 500 runners-up drawn out of the hat will each receive special National Trust Centenary prizes. The winners and runners-up will be notified by post by 31st January 1996.

The Golden Acorn is hidden at ....

The map reference is ....

The secret message is ....

The magic words are ....

My name is ....

My address is ....

.... Postcode............................

Telephone number ....

Age...

Signature of parent/guardian...

This competition is open to all children aged 16 and under on 31st December 1995 (except for children of employees of Penguin Books Ltd).

A full list of the rules of entry can be obtained by sending a stamped addressed envelope to Puffin Books at the above address.

Please tick this box if you do not wish to receive additional information about Penguin Children's Books ☐

SEARCH FOR THE GOLDEN ACORN

The Story

I'm bored!' said Abby, lying on the living room floor, surrounded by a pile of books and comics.

'So am I,' said Charlie, her younger brother.

Just then Mum came into the room. 'Have you got everything ready for tomorrow?' she asked.

'Yes, Mum!' they said together.

'New pens and pencils?'

'Yes, Mum!'

'New batteries in your calculators?'

'Yes, Mum!'

'Blazers nice and clean?'

'Clean-ish!' said Abby.

Charlie looked out of the window. 'I wish it would stop raining,' he sighed. 'Then at least we could go out and play in the park.'

'Cheer up,' said Mum. 'We'll do something special for the last day of the holidays. Come on, I'll get the car out. Charlie, tie your laces. You'll trip yourself up!'

'Where are we going, Mum?' asked Abby when they were whizzing down the motorway.

'Wait and see,' said Mum.

A minute or two later, Mum turned off the road. Charlie saw a sign saying 'Charlecote Park' at the side of the road. 'I didn't know there was a theme park here,' he said. 'I hope there are lots of really scary rides!'

'I don't think it's a theme park, is it Mum?' said Abby.

'No it's not,' replied Mum. 'It's an old house, run by the National Trust!'

'National what?' said Abby.

'National Trust,' said Mum. 'It's an organization that looks after some of the most interesting places in the country. Houses, gardens, and acres and acres of countryside.

'Some of the places they care for are really exciting, like the wall that the Romans built right across the country to keep invaders out. And houses with secret rooms where priests held forbidden services. They could have been executed if they were caught, you know!'

'Wow!' said Charlie.

They had parked the car by this time and were walking towards an impressive gate house.

'Charlie,' said Mum. 'Please tie your laces!'

They went inside. Charlie thought that the house was a bit gloomy. 'Where are the hiding places?' he asked.

'I'm not sure if there are any here,' said Mum. 'Let's ask that lady, shall we?'

'Look Mum,' said Abby, tugging at her sleeve. 'Look at the boy in that picture.' Abby was pointing to a large painting above the fireplace in the Great Hall. 'He looks just like Charlie.'

Intrigued, Charlie and Abby went to look more closely at the portrait. Suddenly Charlie tripped over the loose laces on his trainer. As he fell, he reached out and grabbed Abby's hand to regain his balance, but he only succeeded in pulling her down on top of him. In her panic, Abby grasped a heavy drape and all of a sudden a strong wind began to blow. Charlie and Abby felt themselves being spun round and round and round. And then, just as quickly as the wind had risen, it stopped.

'Where's Mum?' cried Charlie.

'Where are the big flower pots?' asked Abby, for the room had changed completely. The floor, which had been covered with marble tiles, was now bare flagstones. Candles flickered from brass candlesticks, and most curious of all, the table and chairs all looked new.

Suddenly, Abby and Charlie heard footsteps mingled with the sound of laughter. 'Quick, Abby. Let's hide!' cried Charlie. But before they could move, the door at the far end of the room flew open and two children burst into the room. When they saw Abby and Charlie they stopped in their tracks.

Abby and Charlie were dumbstruck at what they saw: a boy and a girl of about their own ages, but dressed in very peculiar clothes. The girl's gown had a square neck, a very narrow waist and a richly embroidered skirt that reached the floor. The boy was wearing knee-length, slashed velvet

pantaloons, silk stockings and a white shirt with frills round the cuffs.

'Who are you?' said the girl.

'And why are you wearing such strange clothes?' asked the boy.

'Strange clothes!' cried a bewildered Charlie. 'This is my best T-shirt, and my jeans were clean on this morning.'

'Sh, Charlie,' whispered Abby. 'Don't you see? They're the children in the picture.'

Charlie stared at the boy and girl. Abby was right. They were the children from the painting.

'What . . . er . . . year . . . is this?' stammered Abby.

'1604 of course,' said the girl. 'The second year of King James's reign.'

'Don't be silly,' said Charlie. 'It's 1995 and Queen Elizabeth is on the throne.'

'Queen Elizabeth!' exclaimed the boy. 'She died last year. But anyway, who are you?'

'I think,' said Abby, 'we'd better explain.'

The two children from the picture listened as Abby and Charlie told them what had happened. When they had finished, the girl said: 'When you fell you must have accidentally set some sort of alchemy in motion that whisked you back to our times. We'd better ask Old Anselm what to do. I'm Abigail, by the way, and this is my brother, Charles.'

'That's funny,' said Abby. 'I'm Abby and this is my brother, Charlie.'

Abby and Charlie followed Abigail and Charles out of the room, along a candlelit corridor, up a twisting spiral staircase and into a round room. There were books everywhere. Piles of them littered the floor. They tumbled along shelves and covered every available surface.

'Anselm?' the boy shouted. 'Are you here?'

His call was answered by a throaty cough. It sent a cloud of dust into the air from behind lots of heavy, leather-bound volumes piled on top of a table.

'Yes. Over here. What is it?' Anselm's voice sounded as if he had just woken up from a snooze. 'I'm busy. Oh, it's you. Go away, Master Charles!'

'But it's important,' said the girl.

'What's important, Mistress Abigail?'

'This boy and girl, Abby and Charlie, have to get back —'

'Get back? Get back to where? Leamington?'

'No, sir,' said Charles, '. . . the . . . er . . . twentieth century.'

'Are you being cheeky, Master Charles? Twentieth century! April the first, is it?' Anselm said angrily.

Eventually Charles and Abigail calmed the old man down and explained Abby and Charlie's predicament. Doctor Anselm huffed and puffed as he listened, and his brow knitted as a curious expression crossed his face. 'It wasn't our fault. Honestly!' said Charlie. 'But please, can we go back to the future?'

'Get back to the future, eh?' chuckled Anselm. 'Well that is a challenge. Makes a change from Lady Lucy's backache!' As he spoke, Anselm began to look for a book. 'Twentieth century,' he muttered to himself over and over again. 'Let me see. What's this? *Basic Helicopter Design* by Leonardo da Vinci. Pie in the sky.' He dropped the dusty volume and picked up another. '*The Time Machine* by H.G. Wells. How on earth did I get that?' he said, setting it to one side and picking up a third. 'Ah,' he sighed. 'This is what I want!'

Anselm flicked through the pages muttering 'Oh,' and

'Hm,' and 'Ah,' as he read. And then, 'Oh dear, oh dear, oh dear!'

'What's the matter?' asked Charles.

'Well,' said Anselm, 'I'm afraid that it's even more of a challenge than I thought.'

Charlie suddenly felt tears welling up in his eyes. 'I want to go home,' he said. 'I want to play with my computer.'

'Your what?' asked Charles.

'Don't you concern yourself with that, Master Charles,' said Anselm. 'Computers are not something you'll ever have to worry about.'

'Now,' he went on, turning to Abby and Charlie. 'Don't be afraid. There is a way. To get back to your own time you need to find the Golden Acorn. When you have it, you turn it round three times clockwise and three times anti-clockwise, then say the magic spell and it will be as if you had never slipped out of your own time at all.'

'Where is it?' asked Charlie desperately.

'Well, I'm afraid that's the problem. I can't tell you where it is. That would be a severe breach of BMA rules.'

'BMA?' asked Abby.

'British Magician's Association,' explained Anselm.

Suddenly Charlie burst into tears.

'Stop blubbering, boy!' growled Anselm. 'I can't be doing with a boy that blubbers. I can't tell you where the Golden Acorn is, but I can point you in the right direction . . . '

'What do we have to do?' asked Abby.

'You must go on a quest. A quest through time and space. At each stop you will be given a puzzle to solve. If you get all the answers right, you will know where the Golden Acorn lies and what the spell is.'

'When can we start?' cried Abby and Charlie together.

'Come here, both of you,' said Anselm kindly, 'and stand beside me.' Anselm put his arms around them, enfolding them in his dusty cloak. He began to spin round, at first slowly, but then faster and faster until with a loud cry he raised his arms and stopped spinning.

With a loud crack and a bright flash Abby and Charlie vanished. Charles and Abigail rubbed their eyes in amazement.

'How very rude,' said Abigail. 'They didn't even think of saying "thank you".'

'But where have they gone?' gasped Charles. 'Can you make us disappear, too?'

'They've gone back a little in time, here at Charlecote, to find their first puzzle,' Anselm said. 'And no. I can't make you move through time. I can only help people who slip out of their own time.'

'What's their time like?' asked Charles.

'Very loud,' said Anselm. 'Very loud indeed.'

❦

CHARLECOTE PARK

Be quiet! And don't move.'

'Who said that?' said Charlie.

'I did.' The voice seemed to be coming from up a tree.

'Where are you?' asked Abby.

'Up here. Hiding from Sir Thomas's steward. If he catches me poaching again, it'll be the stocks or worse for me! Come on up.'

Abby and Charlie scrambled up the tree. And just in time too, for no sooner were they hidden in its thick green leaves than an angry-looking man crept into the clearing, looked around, scratched his head and with a puzzled expression on his face vanished from the children's sight.

Charlie began to climb down.

'Best wait up here a bit,' said the poacher. 'Just in case.'

'Who are you?' asked Charlie.

'Shakespeare's my name. Will Shakespeare.'

'William Shakespeare!' shouted Charlie in astonishment.

'Sh! You'll scare the deer,' whispered Will.

'I can't see any deer,' said Charlie peering down into the bushes below.

'Neither can I,' said Abby.

'Look very closely, Charlie. I think it would be best for you if you could see some,' said Will. 'Be sort of PUZZLING if you didn't!'

'How do you know my name?' asked Charlie. But before Will could say anything, Abby grabbed her brother's arm. 'Puzzling,' she said. 'Don't you see, Charlie? It's our first puzzle!'

'Talk about much ado about nothing!' said Charlie.

'"Much ado about nothing!"' said Will. 'I like that. I must write that down when I get home.'

'Do you write a lot?' asked Charlie.

'No, everyone laughs at my spelling mistakes. They make a right comedy of my errors!'

How many deer can you see?

If you see	Letter	Number	Go to
1	M	3	Brecon Beacons (p48)
2	E	4	Oxburgh (p34)
3	T	5	Beningbrough (p58)

CALKE ABBEY

'Don't touch anything, Charlie,' said Abby. 'You're bound to break it.' The children were standing in a large room, crammed with stuffed animals and egg shells.

'I think it's a bit creepy to stuff dead animals and put them in glass cases,' said Charlie.

'It's called taxidermy,' sniffed Abby.

'I don't care what it's called,' said Charlie. 'They give me the creeps.'

'I know what you mean,' agreed Abby. 'It's the way they sort of look at you with their glassy eyes!'

Charlie looked out of the window and saw, on a hill behind the house, a large square stable block. 'Let's explore,' he said.

The two children ran out of the house and followed a path that led up to the stables.

'Look at those carriages,' cried Abby. 'They're beautiful. Charlie! Come back! Charlie!'

Charlie had run ahead and was clambering into a small, light dog cart. 'Look at me!' he cried, waving his hand up and down like the Queen.

Then he began to jump around making the cart rock violently on its springs. Suddenly, there was a loud creaking and groaning as first one wheel and then another fell off. With a huge smash, the dog cart crashed to the ground with such force that the sides and bottom fell off.

'Don't just stand there with your "I told you so!" expression on your face,' cried Charlie. 'Help me put it back together again.' He looked at the pile of bits and pieces, scratched his head and said, 'But there are too many pieces.'

How many extra pieces are there?

If there are	Letter	Number	Go to
6 pieces	A	4	Hadrian's Wall (p74)
4 pieces	Y	3	Cragside (p120)
2 pieces	H	2	Grasmere (p88)

ABERGLASLYN

'Can I help you?' Abby and Charlie looked around them and saw that they were in a shop. There were books, brochures, maps, and teatowels, keyrings, tins of biscuits - and lots more. Many of them had 'The National Trust' stamped on them.

'Yes, please. Could you tell us exactly where we are?' said Charlie.

'Why, the National Trust Shop at Beddgelert, of course. In Snowdonia. One of the most beautiful parts of Wales,' said the lady behind the counter. 'I was just about to close, but I can stay open for a minute or two.'

'We're sort of looking for a puzzle,' said Abby.

'Got some lovely jigsaws of Snowdon,' said the lady. 'The mountain, not the earl!'

'No, not that sort of puzzle,' said Charlie. 'Thank you.'

'Oh,' said the lady with a twinkle in her eye. 'Another sort of puzzle is it? Follow me then!'

She led them out of the shop and pointed up the narrow street.

'If you go to the end of the village,'

she said, 'you'll find three paths. One of them leads to the grave of Gelert.'

'Who?' said Abby.

'Gelert! He was Prince Llewelyn's dog. And if you don't know that Prince Llewelyn fought the English in the thirteenth century, then I don't know what they're teaching you in school these days!'

Which path leads to Gelert's grave?

If you choose	Letter	Number	Go to
A	L	5	*Allen Banks (p82)*
B	D	6	*Corfe Castle (p116)*
C	O	7	*Clumber Park (p56)*

PLAS NEWYDD

'Finished! Thank goodness for that.' The young man wiped his paintbrush on the smock he was wearing. I hope the marquis likes it!' He stood back and admired the enormous painting that covered an entire wall of the dining room.

'Gosh,' said Charlie. 'That's a painting? It looks really real!'

'Glad you think so,' said the young man. 'You're meant to think that you could step into it. My name's Whistler, by the way. Rex Whistler.'

'I'm Abby and this is my little brother, Charlie!'

'How do you paint like that?' asked Charlie.

'It's a trick, really,' said Mr Whistler. 'It's hard to explain, but it's called *trompe l'oeil*. It means trick of the eye. You can make flat ceilings domed and square rooms look round.'

'What are these?' asked Abby, pointing to some footprints in the painting.

'Ah!' said Mr Whistler. 'The footprints. They were made by . . .' Then he stopped and smiled. 'But there are clues in the picture. You tell me who made them.'

'Did you paint a picture called *Whistler's Mother*?' asked Abby, remembering a visit to an art gallery.

'No,' said Mr Whistler. 'That was another Whistler. But because I whistled such a lot when I was a boy, my mum called me Mother's Whistler!'

Who do you think made the footprints?

If you think it was	Letter	Number	Go to
Neptune	W	5	The Argory (p96)
Mars	G	6	Boscastle Harbour (p60)
Saturn	D	7	Colby Estate (p114)

CHEDWORTH

I hate this country!' The woman's voice was very sharp. 'I don't know why we had to come here. It's cold. It's damp. The slaves are rude. There are no decent shops. I want to go back to Rome. Are you listening to me, Claudius? Write to Caesar and ask for a transfer!'

A moment or two later, a door slammed and Abby and Charlie heard two sets of footsteps on the path outside. They ran to the window just in time to see a man dressed in a toga and a woman wearing a loose, white dress leave the house.

The children were standing in a simple, spacious room. The floor was tiled in marble, and painted pictures covered the walls. Two long, low marble benches were set on either side of a table covered with parchment scrolls.

Charlie picked one of the scrolls up. 'Look, Abby. What language is this?'

Abby looked over his shoulder at the words on the scroll. 'I think it's Latin,' she said.

'There's something very odd here,' said Charlie looking around him. 'If we're in Roman times . . . there's something very odd indeed!'

How many things can you see in the picture which wouldn't have been there in Roman times?

If you see	Letter	Number	Go to
5 odd things	O	5	Alderley Edge (p44)
8 odd things	K	6	Cliveden (p112)
10 odd things	Q	7	Lacock Abbey (p78)

CONISTON VALLEY

'S orry! I didn't see you there, sir,' said Charlie, tripping over the legs of an elderly gentleman. The old man was sitting on the pebble beach beside a beautiful lake set amid hills and craggy peaks.

'Then you should look where you're going, young fellow,' said the man. 'Young people today are in too much of a hurry!'

As they were talking, a boat sailed by. There were four children of about Abby's age on the deck. Deafening music blared from a loudspeaker.

'And some of them are too loud!' the man added. 'When I was young, children used to play quietly. They didn't need all this music to enjoy themselves.' His eyes misted across as he began to remember. 'See that island there?' he said, pointing out to the lake. 'That's Peel Island. I called it Wild Cat Island in my books.'

'Books?' said Abby.

'Yes! *Swallows and Amazons*! *Secret Water . . .*'

'*Swallows and Amazons*!' cried Charlie. 'Then you must be Arthur Ransome! I love your books.'

'Good of you to say so,' said Mr Ransome, getting to his feet. 'Best be going. Best be going.' And he made his way along the beach.

'Look, Charlie,' said Abby, pointing to a piece of paper that lay on the beach where the elderly gentleman had been sitting. 'It must have fallen out of his pocket.'

The two children looked at the paper. On it was a grid filled with lots of letters. There was a message too, written in very shaky handwriting: 'The names of some of the characters from my books are hidden in the grid. How many can you find?'

```
A T I T T Y W A L K E R Q U A D J H
V R I E O D I S S E A Q J R D F O D
I C J I M B R A D I N G K N S W H V
C V P H U R L F D T F E S D C B N R
K A T M R S B L A C K E T T B G W F
Y E Y J F T Y G E U J R E F N T A N
W R U K H V R H Y P V T T L J D L J
A G G C A P T A I N F L I N T X K L
L H H A B U G K U G P H W T K I E D
K Q J S M E H L I N R X N I L O R S
E A K D S T T E P M W S C E E T E X
R U O F R O G E R W A L K E R F E T
W I W R F L U G W E Y O V T I G A O
E O S S U S A N W A L K E R O H T G
O P D T G U I H R F T U E Y P S N U
K I G U K O O I H Z U W T U W X U E
P E G G Y B L A C K E T T D E E I D
W Q H I L F P O J Q O E U G R T R T
R W O U U N A N C Y B L A C K E T T
B H A B J B N U K H P Y J F G U B S
```

If you find	Letter	Number	Go to
5 or 6	E	6	Danbury (p52)
7 or 8	L	7	A La Ronde (p68)
9 or 10	T	8	Runnymede (p106)

ERDDIG

There was a leg of mutton in that baking tray when I went up to discuss this evening's menu with m'lady! And I wants to know who's took it!'

'Calm down now, Mrs Danvers! I'm sure we can get to the bottom of this.'

Abby and Charlie were standing in the kitchen of what must have been a large house, judging from the size of the fireplace, the rows of pots and pans and the enormous black range on which pots bubbled, sending delicious smells wafting round the room.

'I'm hungry,' said Charlie.

'Sh!' hushed Abby. 'I think we'd better stay out of the way.' And she and Charlie slipped beneath the heavy white cloth that covered the wooden table in the middle of the room.

'Mutton doesn't grow on trees, you know!' said Mrs Danvers. 'You marks my words, Mr Hudson. Mutton doesn't grow on trees!'

'Who was here when you was summoned upstairs?' asked Mr Hudson.

'William, the pantry boy. John, the boots. And Mary, the scullery maid,' said Mrs Hudson. 'And the dog was lying by the range. Some guard dog he is,' she went on. 'Erddig could be over-run with burglars and Killer wouldn't budge.'

Killer heard his name, and sat up lazily.

'William! John! Mary!' Mr Hudson's voice boomed around the kitchen. 'Come here, NOW!'

Two frightened-looking lads came out of the pantry, both chewing rather hurriedly, and a sullen-looking girl came into the kitchen from the scullery, banging the door loudly behind her.

'Now then,' said Mr Hudson. 'Someone's stolen Mrs Danvers' —' Before he could finish the sentence, the two boys chorused, 'It wasn't us, sir!' And the girl said, 'Maybe the dog ate it.'

Who do you think stole the meat?

If you choose	Letter	Number	Go to
Mary	R	1	Baddesley Clinton (p84)
The boys	N	2	Castle Ward (p42)
The dog	A	3	Florence Court (p90)

OXBURGH HALL

Excuse me, sir,' said Charlie. 'Can you tell us where we are?'

The gloomy looking man turned round. 'Where we are? Sir Edmund Bedingfeld's place, Ox . . . er . . . Oxfield. No, Oxburgh Hall.'

'Why were you staring out of the window?' asked Abby.

'I'm puzzled,' said the man.

'Perhaps we can help you,' said Charlie.

'On my way here,' murmured the man, 'one of my horses lost its shoes. We stopped at a blacksmith and I asked him how much it would cost me to have it shod. He quoted me an outrageous figure. "Look here!" I said to him, "Just because I'm King Henry VII, doesn't mean I'm made of money, you know."

'"Well then," said the blacksmith. "I'll give you my special rate. We need 24 nails, so I'll charge one groat for the first nail, two for the second, four for the third and so on."

'"Capital!"' I said. And he set to work. When he had finished he gave me his bill. Look. Here it is,' said the King. 'That can't possibly be right, can it?'

Charlie took the bill and he and Abby looked at it carefully. 'I'm afraid it is right, sir — sorry, sire,' said Charlie after a few minutes. 'I think you've been outwitted!'

He was good at arithmetic. His teachers had once told his dad that he was the best in the whole school and Dad had said, 'That doesn't add up with the Charlie I know!' and laughed loudly at his joke. No one else had.

'Disgraceful!' roared the king. 'What sort of blacksmith would do that to a king?'

'A clever one?' suggested Charlie.

How many groats had the blacksmith asked for?

If you think is was	Letter	Number	Go to
6,777,215	N	2	*Brecon Beacons (p48)*
16,777,215	E	4	*Lyme Park (p72)*
216,777,215	F	6	*Bateman's (p98)*

EAVES AND WATERSLACK WOODS

'Look Abby,' said Charlie, pointing to the sea in the distance. 'That looks like Morecambe Bay, where we went on holiday last year.'

'So it does,' said Abby. 'Remember how we buried Dad in the sand and –'

All of a sudden there was a loud rat-a-tat-tat.

'What was that?' Abby said.

'Search me,' said Charlie. 'No, hang on a second. Look – on that tree!'

The two children stared at a tree about three or four yards away. Clinging on to the bark was a beautiful green bird. Its head was bobbing backwards and forwards as it drilled its sharp beak into the wood, looking for insects to eat.

A few minutes later it flew off into a tree close by. 'Maybe that's where its nest is,' said Charlie. 'Let's go and see. There may be eggs or chicks in it.'

'No, leave it be,' said Abby. 'We may scare it away from the nest forever. Let's wait and see if it comes out again.'

A few moments later the woodpecker emerged from the greenery.

'It's got a bit of paper in its beak,' said Abby. The bird flew right up to the children, dropped the paper at their feet and vanished. 'Don't look so disappointed, Charlie,' said Abby. 'What is it Granny says? "Keep your pecker up!"'

Picking up the paper, Charlie grinned, 'Don't you mean "my woodpecker"?'

On the paper it said:

Which one of these birds won't fit into the grid?

Woodpecker	Auk	Wren	Skylark
Owl	Gull	Curlew	Skua
Plover	Swallow	Lark	Duck
Quail	Cockerel	Razorbill	Dove
Hawk			

If you choose	Letter	Number	Go to
Duck	I	7	St Michael's Mount (p62)
Hawk	E	8	Giant's Causeway (p100)
Wren	O	9	Coniston Water (p122)

STEPHENSON'S BIRTHPLACE

Phew! It's hot in here!' said Abby.

They were standing in a cramped, tiny kitchen. A fire was blazing in the fireplace and balanced on the coals was a kettle, with clouds of steam blowing from its spout.

A young boy ran into the kitchen, wrapped his hand in a damp cloth and was about to take the kettle off the coals when he stopped and gazed at it, a curious look on his face. The steam was coming out with such force that it was making the lid bob up and down. Suddenly he saw Abby and Charlie. 'Hello!' he said. 'I'm George. George Stephenson!'

'Abby!' whispered Charlie. 'I think that's the George Stephenson who sort of invented trains!'

'Trains?' asked the boy. 'What are trains?'

Charlie ran round the small room with his arms moving round and round, and shouting, 'Choo-Choo!'

'Is your brother mad?' said George, taking the kettle off the fire.

'Trains . . . Choo-Choo! Hm. Must be off his head!' The boy took the kettle out of the room and left Charlie and Abby alone.

'Funny,' said Abby spotting a postcard on the mantelpiece. 'I could swear that wasn't here when we came in.' She took it from the shelf. 'Charlie!' she cried. 'It's our puzzle!'

Here are two pictures of George Stephenson's Rocket.

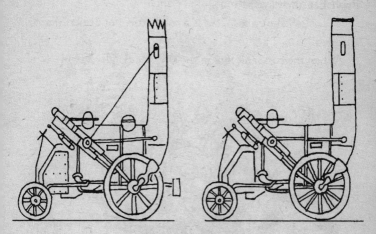

How many differences can you spot?

If you see	Letter	Number	Go to
6 differences	R	3	Florence Court (p90)
5 differences	E	4	Coniston Water (p122)
4 differences	Z	5	Eaves Wood (p36)

BLACKWATER ESTUARY

Wodin!' The blood-curdling cry sent a cloud of waterbirds who had been wading in the mudflats on Ray Island screeching into the air.

'Wodin!' The cry rang out again. A few minutes later hundreds of Vikings were engaged in full-scale battle with an army of Anglo-Saxons.

'Best keep our heads down!' Abby had to shout to make her voice heard above the sound of the battle. She grabbed her brother and pulled him down to the marshy ground.

The battle raged for hours. Abby had to keep a firm grip on Charlie for he kept popping his head up and shouting, 'Pow! Let him have it!'

'Charlie!' she cried. 'This is a real battle, not Super Mario Brothers!'

When the sun sank low in the sky, the Anglo-Saxon

soldiers turned on their heels and ran for their lives. 'Let them go!' cried a huge man, raising a horn-shaped beaker to his lips. 'Come! Let us give thanks to Wodin and Thor for this memorable victory!'

He took a deep draught from the beaker and threw it over his shoulder. It landed with a loud clang on a stone a few feet from Charlie and bounced towards him.

'Look, Abby!' he said, reaching out to grab it. 'There's something carved on it! I bet you it's our puzzle!'

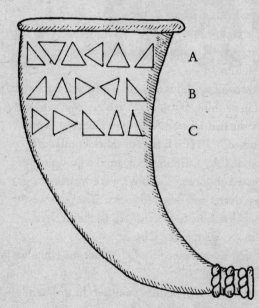

Which row of shapes do you think is the odd one out?

If you choose	Letter	Number	Go to
Row A	D	9	*The Argory (p96)*
Row B	T	8	*Plas Newydd (p26)*
Row C	S	7	*Buckland Abbey (p102)*

CASTLE WARD

N ow if you look up, boys and girls, you will see some
lovely fan vaulting that Lady Anne . . .' She stopped
suddenly, for she had spotted Abby and Charlie. 'You two,'
her voice boomed, 'WHERE is your school uniform?'

Charlie and Abby were standing amid a group of very
curiously dressed children. The boys were wearing bright-red
blazers, baggy shorts and long red socks. The girls were
dressed in shapeless blue tunics that fell to their calves.

'Er . . . em . . .' stammered Charlie.

'Never mind now,' rasped the lady. 'See me when we get
back to the charabanc!'

'I think you look very scruffy,' sniffed the girl beside
Abby. 'MY mother wouldn't let me come to school dressed
like that.'

Abby grimaced and said, 'Well MY mother wouldn't let
me out looking like a sack of potatoes!'

'Miss!' cried the girl. 'That girl said I looked like a sack of potatoes.'

'Quiet!' snapped the teacher. 'Now pay attention. The fan vaulting is based on Henry VII's Chapel at Westminster Abbey, in London . . .'

Suddenly Charlie saw an envelope behind a pillar. On the front was written 'Abby and Charlie.' He reached out very carefully, grabbed the envelope and stuffed it into his pocket. When the others left the room, Charlie and Abby tiptoed away. As they opened the envelope, they heard the teacher say, 'Maris Piper! Pay attention! That child doesn't even know it's 1936!'

Castle Ward was completed in 1770. Which of these assortments of Roman numerals can make that date?

Tablet	Letter	Number	Go to
1	S	3	Black Down (p70)
2	A	4	Cherryburn (p108)
3	I	5	Runnymede (p106)

ALDERLEY EDGE

There was a soft thud as Charlie and Abby landed on the turf at the bottom of a steep wooded slope. Behind them the pastureland was dotted with small copses. 'What a pretty place,' said Abby. 'But it's a bit . . .'

'Spooky!' Charlie shivered as he finished the sentence for her.

'Spooky?' a voice boomed. 'What do you mean, "Spooky?"'

'Who said that?' said Abby.

'I don't know,' Charlie mumbled through chattering teeth.

Suddenly, with an almighty flashing and a banging, an elderly man landed on the ground, right in front of the children, and tripped over onto his back!

He stood up, shook himself and said, 'I'm getting far too old for special effects.' He looked at the children and went on, 'Now you must be Charlie and Abby!'

'How do you know our names?' gasped Abby.

'There is very little I do not know,' said the man. And, seeing the puzzled expression on Abby's face, he went on, 'I am Merlin, court magician to King Arthur and the knights of the Round Table. At least I was, until that bounder Modred stirred up all that trouble and spoiled things. I guard the entrance to one of the caves nearby.'

'Which one?' asked Charlie. 'Can we come and see it?'

'Of course you can,' said Merlin. He waved his hand and one of the rocks nearby glowed like a television screen. Then a picture of a cave with a dog in it flashed onto it. Then the same thing happened to the rock next to it, and the one next to that one too.

'Which one is yours?' asked Charlie.

Merlin smiled, 'That's for you to tell me,' he said. 'But you'll find the answer in a low light.'

Which of the caves is Merlin's?

Cave	Letter	Number	Go to
with the dog	E	6	Anglesey Abbey (p76)
with the owl	D	7	Knole (p86)
with the cat	U	8	Bradenham (p118)

SUTTON HOUSE

'There's something very odd,' said Charlie.

'What do you mean?' asked Abby.

'Well! That girl over there is wearing a Take That T-shirt.'

'So much for her taste in music!' scoffed Abby. 'Has she not heard of Suede or Wet Wet Wet?'

'No! Listen,' said Charlie. 'She's wearing a T-shirt, but that boy over there looks as if he's stepped from the pages of a history book, and that man has a long curly wig on, like Charles II used to wear!'

'Quiet you two,' the man in the wig's voice boomed across the large, panelled room. 'Now let's get on!'

Charlie looked around: an open brochure lay on the table beside him. 'Look, Abby,' he whispered. He had picked the brochure up, flicked through it and stopped at a picture.

'That's the room we're in. Listen! "Sutton House in Hackney is the oldest house in the East End of London, dating from around 1535."

'And look,' he went on, thumbing through the pages, 'there's the man in the funny wig.'

Abby looked. 'It's the Young National Trust Theatre.'

Charlie picked up a programme that had been

under the brochure. 'They're performing something called *Virtues and Vanities*, set in Charles II's reign. That explains the wig.'

'What year is it on the programme?' asked Abby.

'1993. Abby! We're almost back to our own time.'

'We've got to find the puzzle,' said Abby who was looking through the brochure. Suddenly she stopped, and pointed at one of the pictures. 'There it is!' she cried.

'Just when it was getting interesting, too!' said Charlie who was watching the performance. 'When we get back I'm going to join!'

'If they'll have you . . . And if we get back.'

What is the value of X?

If you think it's	Letter	Number	Go to
440	S	1	*Cragside (p120)*
445	E	2	*Calke Abbey (p22)*
450	F	3	*Grasmere (p88)*

BRECON BEACONS

B rr! It's freezing!' Charlie shivered as he spoke. 'Where do you think we are?'

'In the Brecon Beacons, boyo!'

Charlie and Abby jumped, for they hadn't seen the couple behind them. The man turned to the girl and said, 'Come on, Gladys. Best be going if we want to get to the top of Penyfan before lunch. Fancy coming with us?' he added looking at the children.

'No thanks,' said Abby. 'We don't have the right shoes on and anyway, we're looking for a puzzle to solve.'

'A puzzle,' said the man. 'I'll give you a puzzle!' He put his rucksack on the ground, opened it and gave Charlie six photographs. One of them showed a craggy hill, the other five were pictures of a lake with the image of a hill showing in its still, clear water. 'There's a puzzle for you,' he said. 'Which of the five pictures is the correct mirror image of the hill?'

'Gosh,' said Charlie, scratching his head. 'That's something to reflect on. I can see it's not 4 or 5 —'

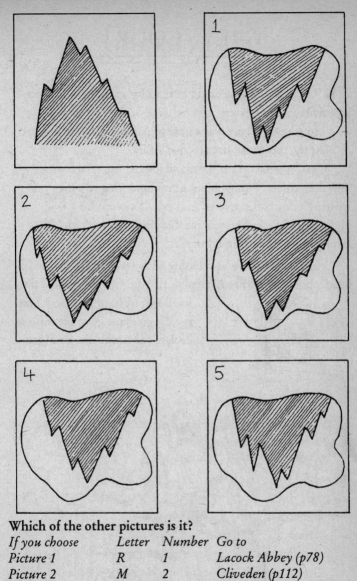

Which of the other pictures is it?

If you choose	Letter	Number	Go to
Picture 1	R	1	Lacock Abbey (p78)
Picture 2	M	2	Cliveden (p112)
Picture 3	N	3	Chedworth (p28)

GREYS COURT

A bby! Where are you?'
'Up here.' Charlie could hear Abby's voice but had no idea where it came from.

'Up where?' There was a note of panic in Charlie's voice.
'At the top of the stairs!' cried Abby.

Charlie raced up the stairs and looked out of the window into the garden. 'I know him,' he said pointing to a man wearing a dog collar around his neck. 'I've seen his photograph in a book we were studying at school. He's the last Archbishop of Canterbury.'

The Archbishop was standing with a pair of scissors in his hand, about to cut through a pink ribbon. Charlie opened the

window just in time to hear him say, 'It gives me great pleasure to declare the Archbishop's Maze open.'

'A maze. I love mazes!' said Charlie.

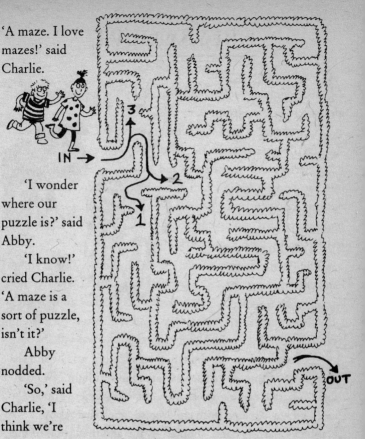

'I wonder where our puzzle is?' said Abby.

'I know!' cried Charlie. 'A maze is a sort of puzzle, isn't it?'

Abby nodded.

'So,' said Charlie, 'I think we're meant to go into it and puzzle our way out. Come on. Let's go.'

'Extraordinary!' exclaimed Abby.

'You mean amazing,' said Charlie.

Which route leads to the exit?

If you choose	Letter	Number	Go to
Route 1	M	6	Arlington Court (p66)
Route 2	E	7	Brownsea Island (p92)
Route 3	C	8	Ashdown Park (p110)

DANBURY

It's very dark!' said Charlie softly.

'Sh!' Abby's voice was little more than a whisper. 'What's that noise?'

The two children stood quite still and listened.

They heard a dog bark in the distance, and then the soft crunch of a footstep.

'I think there's someone coming,' said Abby.

No sooner had she spoken, than a lantern was lit and the two children found themselves bathed in soft light. 'Who's that?' a harsh, rasping voice cried out. 'Stay where you are.'

The voice scared both children so much that Abby grabbed Charlie's hand, shouted 'Run!' and they took to their heels . . . right into the path of a large, black dog whose yellow eyes flashed in the lantern light.

The dog growled deeply.

'Stay, Boney!' someone snapped. 'You two, come 'ere.'

Abby and Charlie walked slowly towards the lantern and found themselves face to face with a good-looking young man whom Abby felt sure she had seen somewhere before. He was wearing a loose white shirt with a frill running down the front. His black trousers were tucked into long, black boots. A sword dangled from his belt. 'Now what 'ave we 'ere? Two little 'uns! Mini excisemen are 'e?'

'Excisemen?' said Charlie in astonishment. 'We're not excisemen! We're only children!'

'Best take 'em with us, Tom!' Another man appeared from out of the darkness.

'You're probably right, Francis,' said Tom.

Abby and Charlie had no option but to follow the two men through the inky blackness of the night across what was obviously rough, muddy grassland.

They walked for what seemed like hours and when they eventually stopped, dawn was just about to break. The man with the sword put his fingers to his mouth and whistled. After a few minutes a tall woman, pulling a heavy cart, appeared.

'Everything loaded, Mary?' the man with the sword asked.

'Certainly is, Captain Cruise!' The woman had a very gruff voice. 'They brought lots of kegs of brandy.'

'And some 'baccy for the parson,' said Tom.

'Best be going then,' said Francis. 'Come on.'

They made their way across the muddy soil, making deep footprints as they went. After a while, they arrived at an inn.

The cart was pulled into a yard and the door firmly locked behind it. Abby and Charlie were forced to help unload the kegs. 'Look Charlie,' whispered Abby suddenly. 'What's written on that label?'

Charlie peered at the label on the barrel and read, 'One of the smugglers is an exciseman on undercover work. Which one?' Suddenly the sound of splintering wood shot through the yard as three customs men broke through the door and arrested two of the smugglers.

'Thank goodness that's over,' said the disguised

exciseman. 'I hate working nights on undercover duty. But I'm looking forward to a good day's sleep.'

'More undercover work,' laughed Charlie. 'The bedcovers!'

Who was the undercover exciseman?

If you choose	Letter	Number	Go to
Mary	C	6	Aberglaslyn (p24)
Captain Cruise	T	7	Allen Banks (p82)
Francis	V	8	Corfe Castle (p116)

CLUMBER PARK

L ook at that avenue of trees!' said Charlie, 'It's so long. It looks as if it goes on for ever.'

'It's the longest avenue of lime trees in Europe,' said a voice.

Abby and Charlie looked around and saw a boy of about Charlie's age. He was sitting in a wheelchair. Stretched out by one of the wheels was a beautiful dog with long floppy ears.

'Hello!' The boy had a warm, friendly voice. 'I'm Luke and this is my dog, Mr Straw.'

'He's beautiful,' said Abby, stroking the dog.

'He's a Clumber Spaniel,' said Luke. 'His ancestors were bred here, by one of the dukes of Newcastle who owned the house that used to be in the park.'

'Do you live here?' asked Charlie.

'Not far away. My mum and dad often bring me here. It's great for people like me. In wheelchairs. There are lots of ramps so I can go all over the park. Come on, I'll show you around. Let's go to the clock tower!'

'That's odd,' said Abby when they got to the clock tower. 'The time on that face is exactly an hour ahead of the time on that one!'

'Ah!' said Luke. 'You noticed. They were wound up at the same time. But one of them is running two minutes an hour

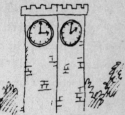

too slow, and the other gains a minute an hour. If you can tell me how long they've been going – then it'll be time for you to go, too!'

'Can't we stay for a bit and explore the park?' said Charlie.

'There's a chapel, and two temples, and a museum,' said the boy eagerly.

'Tell you what,' said Abby. 'When we get back, we'll ask Mum to bring us here.'

'OK,' Charlie agreed. 'Now let's see. One loses two minutes an hour . . .'

How long do you think the clocks have been running?

If you think it's	Letter	Number	Go to
10 hours	A	4	Buckland Abbey (p102)
15 hours	S	5	Blackwater Estuary (p40)
20 hours	R	6	Frensham Common (p64)

BENINGBROUGH HALL

Before you could say 'fish fingers', Abby and Charlie
found themselves in a large room with a very high ceiling.
In the corner there was a chimney-piece, part of which was
made of plates, saucers, serving dishes and bowls of different
shapes and sizes, all made of the most delicate blue and white
porcelain.

'The people who own this must support Chelsea,' smirked
Charlie.

'It's Chinese,' said Abby. 'I know 'cos—'

'Look!' interrupted Charlie. 'That cat!'

The children watched in horror as a black cat jumped up
from a chair onto the bottom shelf and began to pick its way
gingerly through the rows of porcelain. Suddenly it knocked
over a large dish which had been balanced on the chimney-
piece. The plate fell to the floor with a loud crash and broke
into several pieces.

A panic-stricken maid ran into the room. 'Oh no!' she cried. 'Mrs Matlock is sure to blame me and tell the master.' As she spoke she knelt down and picked up the pieces. 'It'll be the workhouse for me unless I can fit it back together again!'

She began to try to fit the pieces together, then stopped. 'That's puzzling,' she said. 'There seems to be an extra piece that doesn't belong.'

'Can we help?' asked Charlie.

Which piece do you think doesn't fit?

If you choose	Letter	Number	Go to
Piece 1	A	4	Oxburgh (p34)
Piece 2	E	6	Chartwell (p104)
Piece 3	N	8	Lyme Park (p72)

BOSCASTLE HARBOUR

Look out, Abby!' shouted Charlie. Too late! His voice was lost in the wind gusting in from the sea, and Abby was drenched in spray as an enormous wave crashed against the rocks.

'You might have warned me!' snapped Abby.

'I tried to,' said Charlie. 'Sorry!'

'I'm soaking,' said Abby. 'I need a towel.'

'There's a cottage or something on that hill up there.' Charlie was pointing at a small whitewashed building on the cliff top.

'It's a look-out tower,' said a voice behind them.

The two children turned round and came face to face with an old man. 'Oh. Thanks,' said Abby. 'Can you tell us where we are?'

'Boscastle Harbour, in Cornwall,' said the man. 'There are Iron Age earthworks near here, and the church nearby was designed by Thomas Hardy.'

'I thought he was a writer,' said Abby.

'That was after. He trained as an architect.'

Charlie hadn't even heard of Thomas Hardy, and didn't care. He was much more interested in the look-out tower. 'Let's go and explore the tower,' he said. 'Thanks for telling us where we are,' he added to the old man.

'You be careful!' said the man. 'These rocks are slippery.' The two children started to clamber along the beach to try to find a path up the cliff to the building. As they walked, the sun came out from behind the clouds. 'Phew! It's hot!' panted Charlie. 'Let's stop for a minute!'

They lay on their backs and enjoyed the warm sunshine which quickly dried Abby. Her annoyance with Charlie soon vanished and she sat up and looked around her. 'Oh look, Charlie!' she said.

Only a few yards away, a colony of grey seals, their fur glittering in the sun's rays, were frolicking on the rocks. The children laughed as one by one the seals began to rise up on their back flippers, seeming to pose just for Abby and Charlie's enjoyment. 'One! Two! Three! Four! Five! Six!' counted Charlie. 'I wonder which way the seventh one will be looking?'

1   2   3

Which seal comes next in the sequence?

If you choose	Letter	Number	Go to
Seal 1	F	6	Colby Estate (p114)
Seal 2	E	5	Sutton House (p46)
Seal 3	O	4	Calke Abbey (p22)

ST MICHAEL'S MOUNT

Welcome, my sons.' The monk smiled as he spoke. ' I've been expecting you!'

'What do you mean, SONS?' Abby was not amused. 'I'm a my daughter, not a my son!'

'Oh dear,' said the monk shaking his head. 'What odd times we live in! What with King Henry threatening to close down the monastery here at St Michael's, and girls who look like boys!'

'St Michael's?' said Charlie. 'Can I have a prawn mayonnaise sandwich?'

'Not that St Michael,' snapped Abby. 'I think he means St Michael's Mount in Cornwall!'

'Quite right, my son . . . sorry, my daughter.'

'That's all right, mother . . . sorry, father,' said Abby. 'Why were you expecting us?'

'Ah,' hummed the monk. 'There are more things in heaven and earth . . . Now follow me!'

Abby and Charlie followed the monk along a torchlit passage into the chapel. 'Now,' he said. 'We are haunted by the ghost of a tall monk. A very tall monk indeed! First you must find him and then tell me what it is in the chapel that matches him in height.'

'Ghost?' cried Charlie. 'Abby, I'm scared!'

'Nonsense,' said Abby. 'Where's your spirit?'

'That's the first thing you've got to find out!' laughed the monk and left the chapel, slamming the door behind him.

What does the ghost match in height?

If you think it's	Letter	Number	Go to
The pulpit	N	6	Coniston Valley (p30)
The font	I	5	Runnymede (p106)
The pillar	E	4	Giant's Causeway (p100)

FRENSHAM COMMON

Hey! You two! What are you doing in there?'

'There's something about that voice that tells me we shouldn't be here,' said Charlie. Holding each other's hand, the two children walked towards the man who had shouted at them.

'Listen!' said Charlie. 'That's a stonechat's call. And that's a nightjar!'

'All birds sound the same to me,' said Abby.

By this time they had reached the man. 'Now then,' he said. 'Can't you two read? Didn't you see all the notices?'

'Why?' said Abby. 'Shouldn't we be here?'

'No!' said the man. 'Now the war's over, we've decided to fill the ponds with water again.'

'Ponds?'

'The Great Pond. And the Little Pond.' The man was talking in the sort of voice that teachers use when they're explaining something to the class dumbo. 'The ones that were drained when the war started so that Gerry pilots couldn't use them as landmarks.'

Seeing the puzzled expression on the children's faces, he said, to no one in particular, 'You would think they didn't even know there's been a war on. This whole area's to be filled with water. But I have to solve this puzzle before I can start. My foreman's a very odd man. Very odd indeed!'

'Perhaps we can help?' said Charlie.

'You can try,' said the man. 'But I don't hold out much hope.'

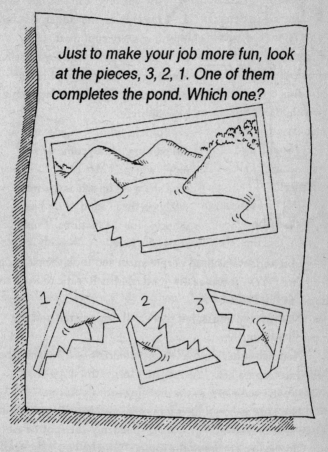

Just to make your job more fun, look at the pieces, 3, 2, 1. One of them completes the pond. Which one?

Which piece completes the boss's picture?

If you choose	Letter	Number	Go to
Piece 1	S	5	Blackwater Estuary (p40)
Piece 2	G	6	Buckland Abbey (p102)
Piece 3	A	7	Plas Newydd (p26)

ARLINGTON COURT

'Now whatever can this be?' said the lady on the ladder, reaching into the pantry cupboard.

'You w— w— watch yourself, Mrs Briggs,' the man holding the ladder stammered. 'This ladder's a bit wobbly.'

'Got it, John! Oh, it's only an old painting. I can come down now,' wheezed Mrs Briggs. 'I must say,' she went on when she was safely on the ground, 'I do like working for the National Trust, especially here.'

John nodded his head in agreement and took the painting from her. 'Yes. It was really good of Miss Rosalie to leave the house to the Trust.'

'Not just the house, but there's all that pewter, and the musical instruments . . .'

'And her father's model ships, hundreds of them there be,' John interrupted her. 'You mustn't forget the ships. And they say the wallpaper in the morning room's unique.'

'Not sure as how I likes it myself,' said Mrs Briggs. 'I like a nice coat of emulsion on a wall!' Suddenly she spotted Abby and Charlie in a corner of the room. 'Who be you?' she said. 'We aren't open to the public yet.'

'Sorry!' said Charlie. 'We were just sort of passing.'

' 'Ere, Mrs Briggs!' said John who had been looking at the picture Mrs Briggs had found in the pantry cupboard. 'I can't see a signature, but I reckon this painting could be valuable!'

'What's that written on the back?' asked Mrs Briggs. 'Looks like some sort of riddle or puzzle.'

John rummaged in his cardigan pocket for his spectacles and peered at the back of the painting. 'Well, I can't make head nor tail of it.'

'Can we have a look, please?' asked Charlie. 'Maybe we can solve it.'

Charlie took the picture and read aloud:

'Take part of a barrow,
A lark and an arrow
And just a bit of a key.
North, South or West?
First East, would be best,
Now you know, or you should. Can't you see?'

'Well, that's easy enough,' he said.

Who do you think painted the picture?

Painter	Letter	Number	Go to
Monet	T	9	Castle Ward (p42)
Blake	N	7	Erddig (p32)
Manet	M	5	Baddesley Clinton (p84)

A LA RONDE

'What a curious-looking building,' said Abby, pointing at the house she and Charlie were standing beside. 'It's round! Do you think it belongs to a witch, like in Hansel and Gretel?'

'It's not round! It's got flat bits,' said Charlie. 'Let's count them.'

Charlie was right! Although the house looked round, as they circled it they counted that it had, in fact, sixteen sides. 'Let's go inside,' said Abby. 'Oh don't look so scared Charlie. There's no such thing as witches!'

They went through the front door and found themselves in the hall. 'It's so big!' said Charlie. 'It must be over 50 feet high!'

'Look,' said Abby, 'that door's open. I wonder what's behind it?'

They went into the room and gasped at what they saw, for the frieze and some of the walls were decorated with feathers! Brown feathers, blue feathers, yellow feathers, red feathers, feathers of all colours were shimmering in the light.

'It's beautiful. When we get home, I'm going to do my bedroom in feathers.'

'Can I have your Wet Wet Wet poster then?' asked

Charlie. But before Abby could answer, a gust of wind suddenly blew through the room and some of the feathers floated down to the floor.

'Best put them back,' said Charlie, picking them up. He looked at the feathers he was holding and looked at the spaces in the pattern. 'But which one goes where?'

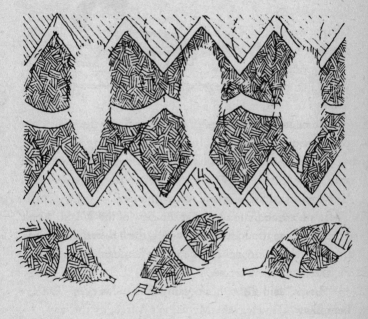

1   2   3

From left to right, which order do the feathers go in?

Order	Letter	Number	Go to
1 2 3	P	6	Corfe Castle (p116)
2 3 1	Y	5	Aberglaslyn (p24)
3 2 1	A	4	Danbury (p52)

BLACK DOWN

'Come into the garden, Fred, now the black, black night has flown . . .'

The man on the grass scratched his head, crossed out the words and started again.

'Come into the kitchen, Fred . . .' Suddenly he was conscious of Charlie and Abby standing watching him, and he put his pen down. 'Hello you two, what can I do for you?' he said.

'Could you tell us where we are, please?'

'Look around you. Look at the view of the Weald. Look at the trees, the rhododendron bushes, the heather. Listen to the pipits, the woodpeckers, the yellowhammer . . .'

'Yes, but where are we?'

'Sussex,' said the man, a dreamy look in his eyes. 'On Black Down. In Heaven! My name's Alfred, by the way. Alfred Tennyson.'

'The poet?' gasped Abby.

'The very same,' said Tennyson.

'I've got a bone to pick with him,' whispered Charlie, remembering having had to learn *The Charge of the Light Brigade* at school.

Abby nudged him to be quiet. 'I think Maud would be better than Fred,' she said to the poet.

'My dear child! What an inspiration! Have you been kissed by the muse?'

'That man's bats!' said Charlie.

'Bats!' cried the man. 'No – bat. Yes that's it.' He picked up his pen and wrote, 'Come into the kitchen Maud, now the bat black night has flown.'

And he got up and walked off, leaving a scrap of paper behind him. Charlie picked it up and looked at what was written on it. 'It's our puzzle, Abby!' he cried.

Alfred's my name
Words are my game
And I have a certain clout,
Look at this list
You should get the gist
Which is the odd one out?

Common   Pharisees
Haggard   Follower
Googly   Noon
Appal   Fellow

Which word do you think is the odd one out?

If you choose	Letter	Number	Go to
Common	A	1	Cragside (p120)
Appal	G	2	Knole (p86)
Fellow	R	3	Hughenden (p94)

LYME PARK

Before you could say supercalif ... superca ... supercalifa ... Julie Andrews, Abby and Charlie found themselves in a room full of clocks. Big clocks, small clocks, square clocks, round clocks, oval clocks, grandfather clocks – almost every kind of clock you could think of.

'I don't like it here,' said Charlie. 'I feel I'm about to be ticked off.'

'Don't be wet, Charlie,' said his big sister. 'There must be another puzzle for us to solve.'

'You're quite right, child,' said a voice. But there was no one else in the room.

'Who said that?' two terrified voices chorused.

'Me of course,' said the voice. 'Oh sorry, I forgot to materialize!' And from out of nowhere there appeared a beautiful lady dressed in medieval robes. 'Don't worry, I'm not going to harm you. I haven't harmed a fly since I died all those years ago. Oh by the way, I'm Blanche. The ghost of Lyme Park!'

'How do you do,' said Charlie who was a very well brought up boy.

'Not so badly – for a ghost, thank you. Now follow me. I have a little puzzle for you to solve.'

She led them into a room. The walls were hung with pictures of dogs.

'Mastiffs,' said Blanche. 'They've been

bred here since . . . let me see . . . about 150 years after I died and that was in 1415. Now, only two of these pictures are identical. Which two?'

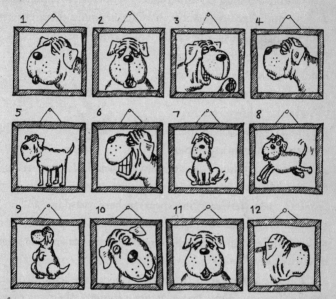

And no sooner had she said the words, than she vanished into the same thin air from which she had appeared.

'I wish I could do that,' said Charlie. 'It would be very handy at school, sometimes.'

Which two dogs do you think are identical?

Dogs	Letter	Number	Go to
4 and 6	R	3	Brecon Beacons (p48)
5 and 8	E	5	Lacock Abbey (p78)
2 and 11	M	7	Bateman's (p98)

HADRIAN'S WALL

A blood-curdling cry filled the air and a large stone whizzed past Charlie's left ear. 'Watch it!' he cried, and then quickly ducked as another stone just missed his right one.

He and Abby crouched behind a large rock and watched in astonishment as a group of men dressed in canvas tunics and with sackcloth wrapped around their feet appeared from a clump of trees not far away. Some of them were carrying spears, others had slings and stones. As they moved towards the high wall that ran as far as the eye could see in either direction, a shower of spears rained down on them.

Charlie looked at the wall and gasped. For standing on the fortifications was a line of Roman soldiers, their breastplates glinting in the sun. The men took to their heels and ran. 'Hm,' grunted Charlie, 'so much for the wild men of the north! Come on Abby, let's go and look at the wall. It must be the one Hadrian had built. It runs right across the country.'

'How do you know that?' asked Abby.

'Mum told us when she was driving us to Charlecote Park. Remember?' said Charlie.

'How could I forget?' said Abby. 'She also told you to tie your laces. Remember? And if you had, you wouldn't have tripped. And if you hadn't tripped, we wouldn't be here now.'

'But just think,' said Charlie. 'If I hadn't fallen over, we wouldn't have met William Shakespeare and the others. And now we've actually just seen Roman soldiers fighting the Ancient Britons.'

'Bit like you and your friends in the playground at break,' sniffed Abby. 'Only the Ancient Britons were better dressed.'

The Roman soldiers had vanished by the time the children reached the wall. 'Look Charlie,' said Abby, pointing at some letters that had been carved on the wall. 'I wonder what they mean?'

Charlie thought for a moment and looked around for a clue. 'Got it!' he said.

What do you think the message says?

If you choose	Letter	Number	Go to
Romans go home	R	4	Greys Court (p50)
Caesar is king	A	5	Brownsea Island (p92)
Kilroy is here	N	6	Runnymede (p106)

ANGLESEY ABBEY

'ood afternoon, sir, madam!' The butler had a very deep
voice. 'His lordship's been expecting you. This way,
please!'

Charlie looked at Abby and shrugged his shoulders. 'Best
do as we're told,' she said, and the two children followed the
butler. 'Isn't that Henry VIII?' asked Abby as they passed a
large portrait hanging on the wall.

'Show off,' whispered Charlie.

'Yes, madam,' boomed the butler. 'It's the earliest known
likeness of him.' He stopped by a very grand door and
knocked before entering.

'The children, sir!' he said and ushered Abby and Charlie
into the room.

'Ah! Welcome to Anglesey Abbey, Abby . . . and Charlie,'
said a cheery-looking elderly man sitting in a large armchair.

'Anglesey!' said Charlie. 'Are we in Wales?'

'No, Cambridgeshire. It takes its name from Angerhale, a village not far from here.'

Charlie looked around the room. Its walls were covered with hundreds of paintings of the same place. 'These are all of Windsor Castle, aren't they?' he said. 'There's hundreds of them!'

'700 or so,' said the old gentleman. 'Now,' he went on, pointing to a space on the wall, and handing Charlie three paintings, 'which of these fills that gap?'

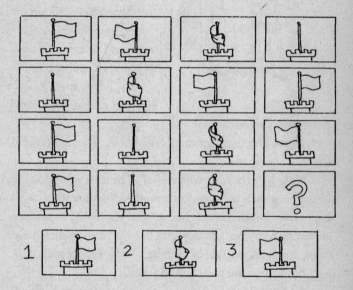

Which picture do you think Charlie should choose?

If you think it's	Letter	Number	Go to
Picture 1	S	4	Stephenson's Birthplace (p38)
Picture 2	R	6	Florence Court (p90)
Picture 3	H	8	Bradenham (p118)

LACOCK ABBEY

I asked you not to move!' The voice was very peevish. 'Now stand still!'

'Best do as we're told,' said Abby, and she and Charlie stood quite still, not moving a muscle.

'I can't keep this up much longer,' mumbled Charlie, trying not to move his lips. 'My left leg's going numb!'

'. . . Fifty-seven, fifty-eight, fifty-nine, sixty! There, you can move now.'

'Thank goodness for that,' said Abby, rubbing her right arm.

'Now let's try somewhere else!' The man who spoke was dressed in a dark tail-coat, cut straight across the front, with an elaborately knotted cravat tied around his neck. His trousers looked to Abby for all the world like ski-pants, with a dark stripe down the outside of each leg. 'Now follow me!'

'Er . . . who are you?' asked Charlie.

'And what's that big box thing you're carrying?' added Abby.

'This?' said the man staggering a little under the weight of the contraption he had tucked under his arm. 'This is my camera. I'm not surprised you had to ask what it is. I've only just made it.'

Just then the housekeeper burst into the room. 'Mr Fox

Talbot,' she cried. 'Your dinner has been on the table for at least half an hour. It's getting cold!'

'Mrs O'Connell, I'm much too busy to eat.' He turned to Charlie and Abby and beckoned them to follow him.

They went along a passageway lined with statues standing in niches in the wall, up a spiral staircase and into a room in a turret.

'What nice carvings,' said Abby looking around. 'Are they very old?

'Hm!' said Mr Fox Talbot, who was tinkering with his camera. 'What? The carvings? John someone did them about three or four hundred years ago. Chapwood was it? No, Chapman. Yes! John Chapman.

'Now, you two. Stand in the corner there. And be very still!'

Abby took Charlie's hand and they stood stiffly to attention for what seemed like hours, until Mr Fox Talbot, satisfied that his picture would be all right, told them they could relax.

'Mr Fox Talbot, if it's your dinner you're looking for when you come down, it'll be in the dog in five minutes!' Mrs O'Connell shouted from the bottom of the stairs.

'Best go,' he said and left the room.

'That doesn't look like a camera to me,' said Charlie walking towards Mr Fox Talbot's machine.

'Abby!' said Charlie, his voice raised with excitement. 'Look! Here's our puzzle.' On the floor beside the camera were four squares of heavy paper. Three of them were perfectly ordinary photographs of Abby and Charlie standing stiffly to attention in the turret room. One of them was the negative. What was black in the photograph was white in the negative and what was white in the photograph was black in the negative.

'Don't we look funny,' said Abby.

'Well, they say the camera doesn't lie!' said Charlie and then read what was written down the side of the negative. 'Only one of these photographs matches the negative: which one?'

'I think,' said Charlie, 'that this is going to develop into something interesting.'

'If this is leading to one of your jokes, Charlie,' said Abby, 'it had better be a good one.'

'I'm positive it will be,' laughed Charlie. 'Get it? Positive. Opposite of negative.'

'Charlie,' groaned Abby. 'Let's get on with it.'

1

2

3

Which photograph was developed from the negative?

If you choose	Letter	Number	Go to
Photo 1	W	6	Anglesey Abbey (p76)
Photo 2	C	5	Knole (p86)
Photo 3	O	4	Alderley Edge (p44)

ALLEN BANKS

'What's that noise?' shouted Abby.

'Sounds like running water!' yelled Charlie.

'Let's go and see. There's a path over there.'

They made their way through the woods until they came to a bridge that spanned a deep ravine. Below they could see fast-flowing water thundering through the deep gorge.

'Look!' cried Charlie. 'There's a deer in the water!'

The two children ran like the wind from the bridge, and crashed through the woods down to the river bank.

'Oh the poor thing,' wailed Abby.

'I'm going in,' said Charlie taking his T-shirt off.

'No, Charlie! The current's too strong!' But it was too late. 'Charlie!' she shouted. 'Come back!'

Charlie was a good swimmer, but the current was very strong and Abby began to worry that he wouldn't make it to the deer, and if he did, he wouldn't be able to swim back to the bank.

Suddenly a man appeared as if from nowhere. He had a length of rope coiled round his waist.

'Don't worry, Abby!' he said. 'We'll soon have him out.' As he uncoiled the rope, it fell in three pieces at Abby's feet.

'Take the longest bit, throw it to Charlie, and haul him in,' he said.

'That was a close shave,' said Charlie a few minutes later when he and the deer were safely on the bank.

'Just as well I happened to be passing,' said the man with a twinkle in his eye.

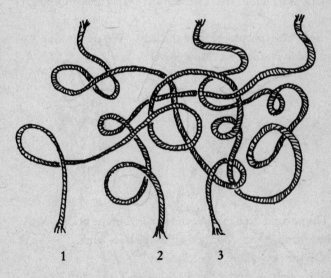

1   2   3

Which piece of rope did Abby throw to Charlie?

If you choose	Letter	Number	Go to
Rope 1	T	6	Clumber Park (p56)
Rope 2	A	7	Blackwater Estuary (p40)
Rope 3	B	8	Frensham Common (p64)

BADDESLEY CLINTON

Nomine Patri. Nomine . . .' But before the priest could finish the benediction, someone burst into the chapel and shouted, 'People coming!'

The priest ran from the altar and disappeared into a side room. No sooner had he vanished than three soldiers ran into the room.

'How dare you!' boomed a very grand lady.

'We've been told that you were holding Roman Catholic services here. You know it's against the law,' said one of the soldiers, as the other two searched the chapel and adjoining rooms.

'Don't be ridiculous!' said the lady. 'We are the king's good and loyal subjects. Now leave!'

'There's no priest here, sir,' said a soldier.

'Hm!' scoffed the officer. 'Very well!' The three men left the chapel.

'But where did the priest go?' asked Abby with a puzzled expression on her face.

'There's a hiding place in the sacristy,' said the lady, who was not at all surprised to see Abby and Charlie sitting in a pew. 'Now why don't you go and see if you can find Father Martin, and tell him it's safe to come out?'

Abby and Charlie went into the sacristy, but there was no sign of any hiding place until Charlie said, 'Oh there it is.' He knocked on the panelling and told the priest to come out.

'I wish I'd listened to my dad and joined the army,' the priest said. 'It's much safer!'

Where is the secret room?

If you choose	Letter	Number	Go to
Behind the fire	Y	7	Cherryburn (p108)
Behind the table	K	6	Black Down (p70)
Behind the cross	M	5	Castle Ward (p42)

KNOLE

Everyone bowed or curtsied as soon as the king entered the magnificent room. He was obviously in a good mood for he smiled and nodded his head as he walked slowly to the huge chair set beneath an elaborate canopy.

'Let it be known,' he wheezed, 'that from now on Knole and all its lands are crown property. I trust there are no objections?'

No one spoke.

'Good!' said the king, and he beckoned Charlie and Abby to approach.

'I hope he doesn't want to marry me,' whispered Abby, stroking her neck.

'Who is he?' mumbled Charlie.

'Henry VIII, idiot!' said Abby, curtsying deeply before the king. Charlie didn't know what to do. He sort of

half-bowed and half-curtsied which made the king shake with laughter.

'Come closer,' he said, and then shouted:

'Master Rich! The coins!'

A tall young man standing by the king presented him with a cushion. On it there were five golden coins glinting in the candlelight.

'How do you like these new coins? They are freshly minted. Splendid, are they not?' said the king. Both children nodded.

'Now look closely, for one of them has an oddness about it that sets it apart from the others. I'd like you to tell me which one.'

'What happens if we make a mistake?' asked Abby.

'We'll toss a coin to decide your fate,' said the king.

'I hope it doesn't come up heads!' gulped Abby.

Which coin does not belong to the set?

If you choose	Letter	Number	Go to
1	Y	10	Stephenson's Birthplace (p38)
2	S	11	Anglesey Abbey (p76)
3	N	12	Bradenham (p118)

GRASMERE

'L ook at all those beautiful daffodils,' said Abby. All around, as far as they could see, there was a mass of golden daffodils weaving and bobbing in the gentle breeze.

'Let's go and look at that lake in the valley,' said Charlie pointing down the hill.

They followed a pebbly path that led downwards through the rough grass. When they were about half way to the lake a man, his brow creased deeply in thought, came up the path towards them and almost bumped into Charlie.

'Look out!' cried Charlie.

The man looked up, startled. 'I'm sorry,' he said. 'I was thinking.'

'What were you thinking about?'

'I want to write a poem but I can't imagine what to write about.'

'How about the daffodils up the hill?' suggested Abby.

'Daffodils!' said the man. 'Nothing rhymes with daffodils. It'll have to be something else.'

'Oh, if you're going to the village could you tell them I'll be late for tea?' he went on as he made his way up the hill.

'Who shall we say you are?' shouted Abby after him.

'Wordsworth!' the man called back. 'William Wordsworth!'

'You've dropped something,' cried Charlie. But the man had gone.

Abby picked up the piece of paper Mr. Wordsworth had dropped. 'Look, Charlie,' she said. 'It's our puzzle!'

'Caffohills rhymes with daddodils,' said Charlie with a note of triumph in his voice.

'There's no such word!' scoffed Abby.

'Isn't that what they call poetic licence?' laughed Charlie.

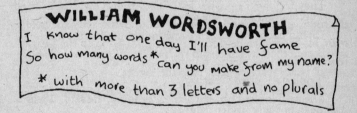

WILLIAM WORDSWORTH

I know that one day I'll have fame
So how many words* can you make from my name?

* with more than 3 letters and no plurals

No. of words	Letter	Number	Go to
10 - 20	O	15	Greys Court (p50)
20 - 30	Y	16	Hadrian's Wall (p74)
30 - 40+	H	17	Cragside (p120)

FLORENCE COURT

Look Charlie! That house. It's on fire!' shouted Abby, pointing to the large, square house not far away.

The two children ran towards the blaze and joined the small group of people standing watching the flames.

'Has someone called the fire brigade?' asked Charlie.

'To be sure,' said a woman nearby. 'As soon as we smelt the smoke, I was on the telephone to the exchange. "Brigit Monaghan," I said, "could you be contacting Brendan O'Grady and tell him to get his men and his fire engines to Florence Court as soon as possible?" And that was at least twenty minutes ago . . .'

She was interrupted by the clanging bells of two ricketty fire-engines roaring up the drive.

'Stand back, everyone!' someone shouted as the men connected their hosepipes to the mains. Within seconds huge jets of water were pouring into the flames.

'I wonder if they'll rebuild it?' said Charlie when the fire had been brought under control.

'Of course they will,' said the lady who had called the fire brigade. 'There's been a Florence Court here since the 1700s. And there'll be a Florence Court here again. You mark my words.'

'Now Brendan O'Grady,' she went on, 'what took you so long?'

'There were roadworks, so we had to take a longer route.' He took a map from his pocket as he spoke. 'We took the Lough Erne Road.'

Charlie looked at the map. 'There's a much shorter road than that,' he said. 'Look!'

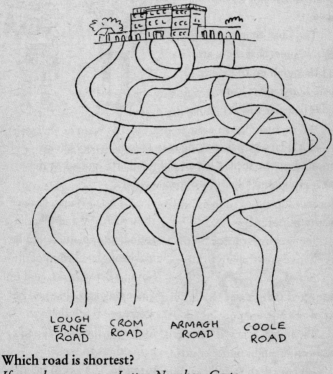

LOUGH ERNE ROAD   CROM ROAD   ARMAGH ROAD   COOLE ROAD

Which road is shortest?

If you choose	Letter	Number	Go to
The Crom Road	M	7	Coniston Water (p122)
The Coole Road	N	8	Eaves and Waterslack Woods (p36)
The Armagh Road	O	9	St Michael's Mount (p62)

BROWNSEA ISLAND

But you're a girl!' said the boy.

'So?' said Abby drawing herself up to her full five feet one inch. 'Is that a problem for you?'

'N. . . no!' stammered the boy. 'It's just that there are no other girls on this camp. I don't know what Lord Baden-Powell will say about it.'

Just then a genial-looking man in long, baggy shorts appeared on the scene. 'It's all right, Albert,' he said to the boy. 'Abby and Charlie are special guests!'

As Lord Baden-Powell showed Abby and Charlie round, he explained that he had brought a group of boys to Brownsea Island on a camping trip. He said he wanted to teach them to look after themselves and to help others to work together. 'I want to help them to be useful members of society when they grow up.'

'Sounds like the boy scouts to me,' said Charlie.

'Exactly, Charlie,' said Lord Baden-Powell. 'Now one of the skills I want to develop in my boys is observation.' He pointed out to a lagoon nearby and said, 'This island is extremely rich in bird life. There are herons, herring gulls, shelduck, curlew, oyster-catchers, dunlin, green shank, and lots more.'

Charlie peered at the lagoon. 'I can't see any,' he said.

'Look carefully, Charlie. And you too, Abby. I want you to tell me how many birds are in and around the lagoon.'

How many birds can you see in the picture?

If you see	Letter	Number	Go to
6 birds	E	4	Arlington Court (p66)
7 birds	A	5	Erddig (p32)
8 birds	D	6	Ashdown Park (p110)

HUGHENDEN

'There's someone coming,' whispered Abby. And no sooner had she spoken than a man opened a door at the end of the passage. He strode across the highly polished floor towards a wall covered with portraits. He gazed at the paintings and then stared at the one he had been carrying under his arm.

Charlie cleared his throat. The man turned and saw the two children. His hair was brushed forwards into a curl that lay on his brow, and he was wearing a primrose in his buttonhole. 'Be with you in a minute,' he said. 'Once I've solved this puzzle!'

'What's that?' asked Abby.

'Well, I found this portrait in the attic. And I can't decide

whether it's one of my Disraeli ancestors, one of my wife's Wyndham-Lewis relations, or one of that rascal Gladstone's people.'

'Disraeli!' exclaimed Abby. 'Are you Mr Disraeli? The Prime Minister?'

'Me? Prime Minister? That's my ambition,' said Mr Disraeli. 'But how could you know that?'

'It's a long story,' said Abby.

Charlie and Abby looked at the portraits and the picture Mr Disraeli was carrying.

'I think it's a Disraeli!' said Charlie.

'I think it's a Wyndham-Lewis,' said Abby.

'I'm sure it's a Gladstone,' said Mr Disraeli.

Who do you think is right?

If you choose	Letter	Number	Go to
Charlie	E	9	Charlecote Park (p124)
Abby	N	8	Charlecote Park (p124)
Mr Disraeli	A	7	Charlecote Park (p124)

THE ARGORY

'I think we must be in Ireland,' said Charlie, listening to the soft, lilting voice of the guide. She was pointing out the glorious barrel organ standing in a marble-walled room.

'It's a bit stuffy in here,' said Abby. 'Let's go outside.' It wasn't really stuffy, but she knew that given half a chance Charlie would turn the handle and probably break the music machine.

The house overlooked a river some distance below.

'Shall we go and see it?' suggested Charlie.

The two children found a footpath that led down to the river. Flowers grew all over the banks of the drainage ditches Abby and Charlie passed. The soft breeze made the flowers weave and bob around like puppets, creating a beautiful tapestry of vivid, changing colours.

Suddenly something flashed in the air. Then there was

another flash and another, as three enormous dragonflies whizzed by. They were quickly followed by two more.

'Abby,' said Charlie. 'What do you call a dragonfly that weighs a ton and breathes fire?'

'Anything it wants!' said Abby. 'I told you that joke last week.'

And then, as if by magic, the five dragonflies stopped and hovered in the air in two lines. Both children were startled to hear a soft voice in the breeze whisper, 'Can you put the dragonflies in the right order?'

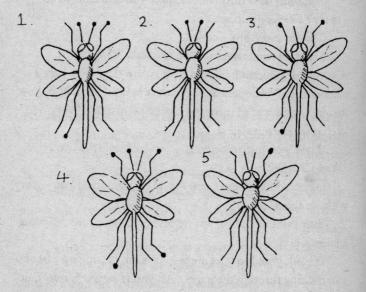

What is the correct order?

If you think it's	Letter	Number	Go to
13542	F	6	Sutton House (p46)
52314	E	7	Boscastle Harbour (p60)
42153	G	8	Colby Estate (p114)

BATEMAN'S

Then you'll be a man, my son,' the man said aloud as he wrote. He was sitting at the large desk in the corner of a bright, sunny room. He put his pen down and picked up a pipe from a rack by his side. Then he spotted Abby and Charlie in the corner. 'Hello you two,' he said. 'Come to see your Uncle Rudyard, have you?'

'Best say yes,' Abby whispered to Charlie. So Charlie nodded and said, 'Yes.'

'Capital!' said the man. 'I expect you'd like me to tell you a story? Everyone does.'

Charlie and Abby nodded.

The man rummaged around his desk. 'Odd,' he murmured to himself. 'Could have sworn they were here a moment ago.' He opened the drawers in his desk, rifled through what was in them and closed them again. 'Very odd. Well, that is a puzzle.'

'Have you lost something . . . er . . . Uncle Rudyard?' asked Charlie.

'My reading glasses,' said the man. 'Can't read you a story without them, can I?'

'But there are lots of spectacles here,' said Abby, handing a pair to him.

'Thank you. Now let me see,' he said, picking up a book and flicking through the pages. 'Ah yes. *How the Camel Got Its Hump*.'

'Charlie!' said Abby. 'I think it's Rudyard Kipling.'

'Who's Rudyard Kipling?' asked Charlie.

'He wrote lots of books,' explained Abby. 'There was *Just So Stories*, *Stalky and Co.* and *The Jungle Book*.'

'I thought that was Walt Disney,' said Charlie.

'Don't you know anything?' Abby asked.

'I know that I'm hungry, and I wish this was the Mr Kipling who makes the cakes.'

How many pairs of glasses can you see in the room?

If you see	Letter	Number	Go to
3 pairs	B	6	*Brecon Beacons (p48)*
4 pairs	H	7	*Chedworth (p28)*
5 pairs	I	8	*Cliveden (p112)*

THE GIANT'S CAUSEWAY

I know where we are,' cried Charlie. 'It's the Giant's Causeway! Finn M'Coul built it for giants to cross from Antrim to Staffa in Scotland.'

'Nonsense!' Abby scoffed. 'It was made millions of years ago by natural forces.'

'The trouble with you, Abby,' said Charlie, 'is that you've got no imagination!'

'No, but *he* had. I recognize him from pictures in books!'

Charlie looked at the man Abby was pointing to. He was dressed in nineteenth-century clothes. 'Who is he?'

'Sir Walter Scott. We must be in the nineteenth century.'

The two children walked over to Sir Walter who was scratching his brow and staring at the honeycomb of hexagonal columns.

'Good morning, sir!' said Abby. 'I've read one of your books, *Ivanhoe*.'

'Well goodness gracious me,' said Sir Walter. 'That's puzzling because I haven't finished it yet. You must tell me how it ends!'

So Abby told him everything she remembered.

'Thank you very much,' said Sir Walter, when she had finished. 'That's saved me a lot of work. I was really puzzled about how to end it.'

'But there's something else that's puzzling,' he went on, pointing to the rocks. There was a number on all but three of the hexagons. 'Now,' he said, 'I can't work out what numbers a, b and c stand for. Can you?'

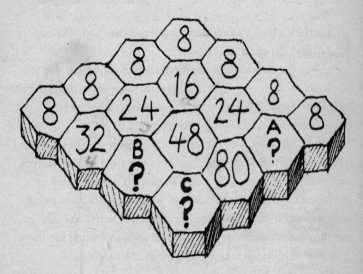

If you think it's	Letter	Number	Go to
a=80, b=160, c=32	S	10	*Runnymede (p106)*
a=160, b=32, c=80	N	12	*A La Ronde (p68)*
a=32, b=80, c=160	T	14	*Coniston Valley (p30)*

BUCKLAND ABBEY

Charlie's scream would have wakened the dead. 'Look, Abby!' he shouted. 'Look!'

Abby peered through the dusk and screamed too, for a black coach drawn by four headless horses was bearing down on them. Running in front of it were twelve goblins, and from behind the sound of baying hounds could be heard.

'Run, Charlie! Run for that house over there!' They ran like the wind to a large rambling house nearby and hammered on the door. 'Come on!' cried Charlie. 'It's getting nearer!' He heard footsteps in the hall, and the sound of chains being pulled back. The heavy door opened and Charlie and Abby ran into the house, where an old woman was waiting for them.

'Sorry!' Charlie was panting hard. 'But we've just seen . . .'

'Sir Francis Drake's coach, I expect,' cackled the old lady.

'The man who beat the Spanish Armada?'

'The very same!' said the old woman. ' 'Tis said he sold

his soul to the Devil for his help to beat the Spanish. This was his house!' The old woman beckoned the children to follow her down a flagstoned passage into a candlelit room. In the corner lay a drum. 'That be Drake's drum! Whenever England is in need of aid, Drake's ghost can be summoned by beating that drum!'

'We could have done with that for the World Cup,' said Charlie.

'Look closely at the drum,' said the woman. 'I think you'll find something puzzling on it.'

Charlie peered at the drum and saw a curious pattern on it. 'It's our puzzle, Abby. It says, "What is the value of the question mark?"'

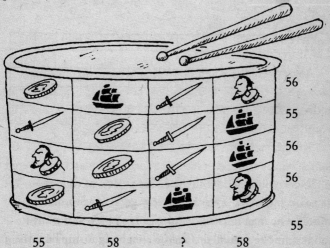

	Letter	Number	Go to
If you think it's			
50	C	6	*The Argory (p96)*
52	T	7	*Plas Newydd (p26)*
54	N	8	*Boscastle Harbour (p60)*

CHARTWELL

'You, boy! Hand me that brick!'

Charlie looked around and saw a fat little man smoking the biggest cigar he had ever seen. 'And tell that girl there to run to the house and tell Clemmie I'll be in for lunch soon.'

'Yes, sir!' gulped Abby, as Charlie picked up a brick from the pile and handed it to the man. He smeared it with cement, placed it at the end of the top row, knocked it with his trowel and then sat down on the grass beside Charlie.

'Now young fellow-my-lad,' his voice was little more than a deep growl. 'I was never very good at arithmetic at school.' The man inhaled on his cigar and blew out a huge cloud of smoke that made Charlie cough. Ignoring him, the man went on, 'I want to build another wall, twice as long as this one and twice as high. How many bricks will I need?'

Just then, Abby came running from the house. 'Excuse me, sir,' she panted, 'but your wife said to tell you there's a 'phone call. King George wants to talk to you!'

'And about time too,' wheezed the man and made his way to the house.

'Do you know who that was?' said Abby. 'Winston Churchill! He's going to be prime minister!'

'Hm.' Charlie's grunt told Abby that he was far from impressed. 'I don't mind if smoking damages *his* health, but I don't see why it should damage mine too!'

How many bricks do you think will be needed?

If you think it's	Letter	Number	Go to
120–130	Y	3	Bateman's (p98)
130–140	T	4	Lyme Park (p72)
140–150	S	5	Oxburgh Hall (p34)

RUNNYMEDE

This is treason!' thundered the king. 'You cannot force me to put my seal to this document!'

'Sire,' said one of the men standing nearby. 'If you refuse, the barons will cause civil war and you will probably be dethroned.'

'That must be King John!' whispered Abby to Charlie. They were hiding behind a tree, trying to keep out of the way of the angry-looking men standing around the king, who looked furious.

'Is that the Magna Charta, then?' said Charlie softly.

'It must be.'

'Oh very well!' said King John. 'But you won't get away with this,' he went on, plunging his great seal into a bowl of hot wax and then affixing it to the bottom of the Magna Charta.

'Gosh! Imagine seeing King John seal the Magna Charta,' said Abby some time later when everyone had gone and she and Charlie were lying on their backs enjoying the sunshine. 'I can't wait to tell everyone when we get back to our own time!'

'If you think anyone's going to believe all this, you're madder than you look.'

'But it's true,' said Abby.

'I know that! And you know that! But try telling anyone else that.'

'Come on. Let's look for our puzzle, now everyone's gone.'

They looked around for a while but saw nothing in the least bit puzzling, until Charlie happened to glance at a signpost by the side of a path by the river. 'There it is, Abby. Come on!'

How many miles is it to London?

If you think it's	Letter	Number	Go to
20	O	6	*Aberglaslyn (p24)*
22	R	5	*Danbury Common (p52)*
24	H	8	*A La Ronde (p68)*

CHERRYBURN

'I love farms,' said Abby. 'Especially the animals.'

'I like the pigs. Oink! Oink!' grunted Charlie, and then he said, 'I'm thirsty! Do you think if we asked at the farmhouse, they'd give us a glass of milk?'

'Let's ask,' said Abby. The two of them walked across the farmyard and knocked on the door. It was opened by a plump, friendly-looking woman.

'Of course,' she said when Abby asked for a drink. 'You'd better come in.'

The kitchen was cool, despite the fire in the huge range that stretched along one wall of the room. The young man sitting beside it was holding what looked to Abby like a pen, and he was scraping it across a block of wood balanced on his knee.

'What are you doing?' asked Abby.

'I'm engraving this wood to make a printing block,' said

the man. 'When it's finished, I'll ink it over and press it onto paper to make a picture.' He pointed to an illustration hanging on the wall. 'There's one I made earlier,' he said, laughing. 'Why don't you and your brother go and have a look at it?'

Abby and Charlie gazed at the beautiful black and white picture. 'It's our puzzle,' said Abby. 'Oh thank you, Mr . . . er . . .'

'Thomas Bewick!' said the man, standing up. The children could see that he had been sitting on a cushion made of rough, prickly-looking cloth.

'Oh look,' laughed Charlie. 'Bewick on Tweed!'

If you use the first letter of each of these animals, you can spell the name of something. What is it?

If you think it's	Letter	Number	Go to
A country	W	3	Black Down (p70)
A town	U	2	Coniston Water (p122)
A planet	R	1	Hughenden (p94)

ASHDOWN PARK

What are you looking for?' asked Charlie.

The man put down his metal detector and looked up. 'Iron Age remains,' he said.

'Why should there be any here?' asked Charlie.

'Because the paths up on the Ridgeway date back to prehistoric times.'

'Have you found anything yet?' asked Abby.

'A ten pence piece and the top set of someone's dentures!'

'How far does the Ridgeway go?' asked Abby.

'It starts in Avebury and runs across the Berkshire Downs, past Ashdown House – that's the little house down there – and on through Oxfordshire. The Ridgeway path for ramblers goes into Hertfordshire.' As he talked, the man picked up his metal detector and swung it backwards and forwards above the ground.

Suddenly there was a loud bleeping sound. The man put the detector down and began to dig. 'Yes!' he cried excitedly, as his trowel hit something hard. But when he reached down to see what it was the triumphant expression on his face quickly changed to one of despair.

'What have you found?' asked Charlie.

'These,' said the man, holding up a scrap of paper and the bottom set of a pair of dentures!

'Is there anything on the paper?' asked Abby.

'It says, "Dear Abby and Charlie..."'

'May we see it please?' asked Abby.

'If it's a puzzle, we'd better get our teeth into it!'

How many times can you see the word iron in the grid?

If you see it	Letter	Number	Go to
4 times	R	12	Erddig (p32)
6 times	U	10	Arlington Court (p66)
8 times	A	14	Baddesley Clinton (p84)

CLIVEDEN

'What a curious building!' said Charlie.

'It's a Chinese Pagoda,' said one of the ladies who were gazing at the tall, ornate structure.

'It looks very out of place here,' said Abby.

They were standing in the gardens of a beautiful house. The house was set high on a terrace some distance away.

'It was built for the Paris Exhibition . . .' another plump lady said.

'In 1867!' said the third.

'How did it get here?' asked Charlie.

'To Cliveden? Maybe the Astors bought it. They were rich enough,' said the first lady.

'No, Doris,' said the second. 'I think it was here before the Astors came over from the States. The Duke of Sutherland, who owned the house before the Astors bought it, must have had the pagoda put here.'

'You're wrong, Mabel,' said Doris.

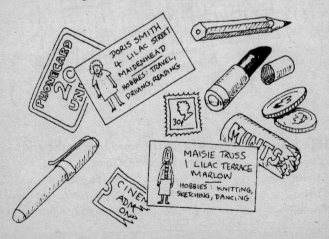

'I AM NOT!'

'Come on now girls,' said the third lady. 'Let's not squabble. Let's go and have a cuppa!'

'Good idea, Maisie!' said Doris and Mabel together and the three ladies walked away.

'Oh look,' said Charlie some time later when they had thoroughly examined the elaborate pagoda. 'One of the ladies has left her bag.' He picked it up, but it burst open and the contents spilled out.

As he and Abby began to put them back in, they noticed three photographs, one of each lady, with some facts about them scribbled underneath. And just then, a piece of paper fluttered to the ground from the pagoda. Written on it was: 'To which lady does the bag belong?'

Who do you think the bag belongs to?

If you think it's	Letter	Number	Go to
Doris	A	7	Lacock Abbey (p78)
Mabel	H	8	Knole (p86)
Maisie	E	9	Alderley Edge (p44)

COLBY ESTATE

I t's very dark in here!' said Charlie. '. . . in here . . . in here.'
His words echoed all around.

'No, there's a glimmer of light over there,' said Abby.
'. . . over there . . . over there.'

'There's a wall here,' said Charlie. '. . . wall here . . . wall
here.'

Abby and Charlie felt their way along the wall towards
the speck of light, which got bigger as they approached it.

After what seemed like hours, they found themselves in a
valley, dotted here and there with abandoned mineworkings.
'Be careful, Charlie,' warned Abby. 'I'd hate you to fall down
a mineshaft!'

'I'm sure they're all sealed. But it would be fun to explore
a mine!'

No sooner had he spoken than he and Abby found themselves deep underground sitting on a cart filled with coal, whizzing along a railway. Suddenly it stopped, and the driver turned round and looked at them.

'What's wrong?' asked Charlie.

'It's this map,' said the driver, handing Charlie a crumpled piece of paper. 'It's my first day on the job and I can't decide which route to take. The rail twists and turns and goes underneath itself. But I think we should go straight ahead.'

'I think we go left,' said Abby.

'No! We go to the right,' said Charlie.

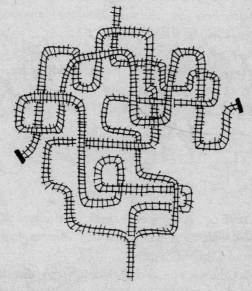

Who is correct?

If you think it's	Letter	Number	Go to
The driver	A	6	Calke Abbey (p22)
Abby	S	7	Grasmere (p88)
Charlie	E	8	Sutton House (p46)

CORFE CASTLE

In the name of General Cromwell, I order you to surrender!'
'Never!' shouted one of the men on the battlements of the great castle. 'The royalist flag will fly from this tower for as long as King Charles lives.' With that, he moved to go back into the Great Hall. Just in time, for no sooner had he slammed the door behind him than a cannon ball landed with a mighty thud right where he had been standing a few seconds before.

'Gosh! That was a close shave!' gasped Charlie.

'It's nothing!' said one of the men. 'We're used to it. We've been under siege now for months. But we shall never surrender to Cromwell's men!

'In fact,' he went on, 'I shall fly another royalist standard from the flagpole. That'll show the bounders!' He began to rummage in a vast oak chest. 'Odd,' he said. 'I could have sworn it was here.' He thought for a moment or two and then it dawned on him. 'Of course,' he said. 'The children were playing with it last week. I wonder where they put it?' He scratched his head and mumbled, 'Puzzling. Very puzzling.'

'Can we help you look?' asked Abby.

'Of course, my dear child! And if you find it you can help me run it up the flagpole.' As he spoke, a cannon ball shattered the glass of one of the windows in the Hall.

'I think we'll just help you find it,' gulped Charlie. 'And then we must be going.'

In which part of the room is the flag?

If you think it's in	Letter	Number	Go to
Part A	E	6	Allen Banks (p82)
Part B	C	8	Clumber Park (p56)
Part C	K	10	Frensham Common (p64)

BRADENHAM

'I know a bank where the wild thyme grows . . .'

'Cut!' An angry voice bellowed across the meadow. 'Hugh, lovey, you're meant to be Oberon, King of the Fairies. You sound as if you're advertising cough medicine. Now try again.'

A girl with a clapper-board appeared, lifted the top bit, snapped it down and said, 'Midsummer Night's Dream! Act 2, Scene 1, Take 356!'

Charlie and Abby were fascinated.

During a break, they asked the director why he had chosen Bradenham as a setting for his film.

'Bradenham,' he drawled, pronouncing it Braden*ham*, 'is perfect. The woods are crammed with beech trees, and the meadows are carpeted with flowers. I mean, look at these primroses, and that wood anemone! It's perfect. The only drawback is all these butterflies!'

'I like butterflies,' said Charlie.

'Don't get me wrong, kid. So do I. But they sure can spoil a close-up.

'Now back to work! Can someone find Emma . . .'

They found the star of the film enraptured by six beautiful butterflies hovering around a bank of bluebells. 'We're waiting for you, Em, sweetie!' cajoled the director.

'I've got to sort these butterflies into three pairs before I can act another word. I'm sorry, darling. I don't know why, either. But I simply have to!'

'Actors!' snapped the director. 'Who needs them?'

'You?' said Charlie. 'Sorry! Just joking!'

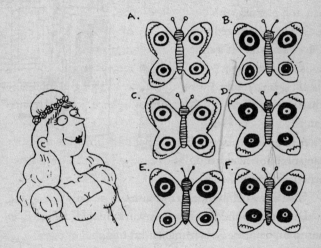

Which butterflies make three pairs?

If you choose	Letter	Number	Go to
AE/BF/CE	R	6	Florence Court (p90)
AC/DF/EB	I	8	Stephenson's Birthplace (p38)
AF/DE/BC	O	4	Eaves and Waterslack Woods (p36)

CRAGSIDE

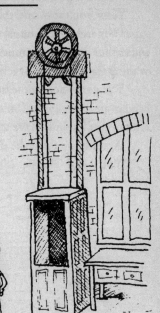

It works!' The man turned the tap on and off, obviously delighted when the water flowed and when it was cut off.

'Looks like an ordinary tap to me,' said Abby to Charlie.

'Nonsense,' said the man, too pleased with himself to be irritated by Abby's remark. 'It's all thanks to hydraulics!'

'Hy-what?' asked Charlie.

'Hydraulics! Using water to produce energy. Too complicated to go into now. But I love it!

'I've designed hydraulic machines to pump water to the house. The lifts and dumb waiter work by hydraulics. Even that spit over there goes round and round thanks to hydraulics. And the house is lit by hydro-electric light.'

'You'll be telling us next that the 'phones work by this hydrowhatsits!' said Abby.

'Phones? No! Of course not! They're mostly for talking room-to-room. If you want to make an outside call, you'll have to use the one in the hall.'

'Phone home?' asked Charlie.

'Not possible,' said Abby, looking at the calendar on the wall. 'Mum hasn't been born yet!'

'Now you two,' said the man, giving them a piece of paper. 'Here's a plan of part of the system. If I turn the tap, where will the water come out? In the kitchen, the bathroom, or the bedroom?'

'What are the black lines across some of the piping?'

'Stopcocks. The water can't get through them.'

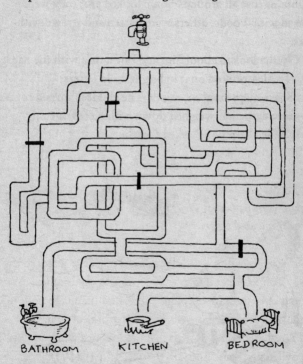

BATHROOM   KITCHEN   BEDROOM

Where do you think the water comes out?

If you think it is	Letter	Number	Go to
In the kitchen	T	5	Brownsea Island (p92)
In the bathroom	A	6	Hadrian's Wall (p74)
In the bedroom	B	7	Greys Court (p50)

CONISTON WATER

Have we been here before?' asked Charlie.
'I can't remember. But I do know we haven't been on a boat before.'

Abby and Charlie were standing on the deck of a yacht steaming along a beautiful lake. Steep hills and majestic mountains rose all around. Some looked as if they were covered with woods, others were barren and strewn with rocks.

Charlie looked about him and saw a ring with the name *GONDOLA* printed on it in bright, bold letters.

''Scuse me, young sir, miss!' The children turned round and saw a carpenter weighed down with pieces of tiling.

'Can we help you?' asked Charlie.

'Well if you could take some of these fro.
most grateful,' said the man. 'I'm Jacob Hamme.
ship's carpenter. Got a little mending to do. You ca.
you like.'

Charlie and Abby helped the man put the tiles on the
deck. Jacob looked at them and scratched his head. 'Well, I
can't make heads nor tails of it!' he said.

'What's the problem?' asked Charlie.

'Well, I've got to make a square out of part A and two of
the other bits. But I can't see which ones to use.'

Which two pieces should Jacob use?

If you choose	Letter	Number	Go to
1 and 4	H	6	St Michael's Mount (p62)
2 and 5	G	4	Coniston Valley (p30)
3 and 6	O	2	Giant's Causeway (p100)

CHARLECOTE PARK

Charlie and Abby looked around the room. 'But we've been here before,' said Charlie. 'This is Anselm's room at Charlecote Park . . .'

'So you made it! Well done, well done,' a voice wheezed from behind a pile of books.

'Anselm!' exclaimed Abby. 'We've had such fun!'

'I know all about it.' Anselm smiled as he spoke. 'And now that you've solved all the puzzles, the Golden Acorn is almost in your grasp.'

'We know roughly where it is,' said Charlie.

'Well,' said Anselm, 'in this envelope there's a little riddle that will tell you exactly where it is. As soon as you solve it you'll be whisked to where the Acorn is. Then you must turn it three times clockwise and three times anticlockwise, say the magic words five times, and you'll be back in your own time.'

As soon as Anselm had given Charlie the envelope, he raised his cloak and began to spin round and round, slowly fading from view as he turned. 'Goodbye Charlie! Goodbye Abby,' he called, his voice floating around the room.

'Goodbye Anselm . . . and thank you,' said the children. Suddenly a thought struck Abby. 'Anselm!' she cried, a note of panic in her voice. 'Before you vanish completely, what are the magic words?'

'L . o . . o . . . k   i . . n . t . h . . e   e . n . . v . . . e . . . . l . . .'
And as he spoke Anselm and his voice softened into nothingness.

Abby opened the envelope and two pieces of paper fell to the floor. She picked up the first and read,

'My first is in sight but not in site,

My second's the third in the word
    neolite.
My third's the middle of the end,
My fourth's the end of a very good
    friend.
My fifth's my second once again,
My sixth sounds like 'the' in the
    language of Spain.
And my seventh . . . comes once in
    Dennis the Menace.'

Charlie picked up the second bit of paper. 'Listen to this, Abby,' he said.

'When you solve my neat little riddle,
Open the door and stand in the middle.
Say aloud the year you were born,
And you'll be with the Golden Acorn.
The magic words you need to be told,
All I will say, is just think bold!'

Abby and Charlie read the two pieces of paper over and over again, until suddenly Charlie said, 'Got it! Come on, Abby. It's time to go!'

☆   ☆   ☆

'Look Mum,' said Abby, tugging at her mother's sleeve, 'Look at that boy in the picture.' She was pointing to a large painting above the fireplace in the Great Hall. 'He looks just like Charlie . . .'

ABOUT THE NATIONAL TRUST
1895–1995

The National Trust is 100 years old in 1995. It owns and protects:

- over 590,000 acres of beautiful countryside
- nearly 550 miles of outstanding coast
- over 300 historic houses, great and small
- over 150 gardens

Wherever you go in England, Wales or Northern Ireland, you will be close to land protected by the National Trust. The National Trust is an independent charity which cares for both the built and natural environment. This includes forests, woods, fens, farmland, downs, moorland, islands, archaeological remains, nature reserves, historic houses, gardens and even villages. It also includes many animals which live on Trust land, and even in Trust buildings – barn owls, red squirrels, natterjack toads, seals, dormice, bats, puffins and many other animals, birds and insects are cared for by the Trust's Wardens.

The National Trust is committed to providing welcoming, worthwhile and enjoyable visits for children and families. Many National Trust properties have children's guide books, there are often children's menus available in the restaurants, and many properties have special events for families and children. Family Group Members also receive *Trust Tracks*, the newsletter for young members of the Trust, giving them news, features, competitions and information on things to do and places to visit.

Join the National Trust in Centenary year

- If you join the National Trust you will be helping us to protect and care for well-loved countryside and coast as well as important historic houses and gardens. Your subscription goes directly to support this work.

- **Benefits of membership:**
  Family Group membership costs just £46 and gives one card covering two parents or partners and their children under 18 living at the same address. This card gives free admission to National Trust properties in England, Wales and Northern Ireland, and to properties in the care of the National Trust for Scotland. Members also receive three mailings a year, providing up to date information on places to visit as well as national and local activities, *The National Trust Magazine* and *Trust Tracks*.

- **How to join:**
  Simply complete the Family Group membership coupon overleaf and return it, with payment of £46, to the FREEPOST address given.

FREE ENTRY VOUCHER

ADMIT ONE ONCE ONLY

The National Trust, 36 Queen Anne's Gate, London SW1H 9AS
'SEARCH FOR THE GOLDEN ACORN'

CHILD ADMISSION (aged 18 or under on 1 April 1995: evidence of age may be requested)
This voucher admits the holder free to one National Trust property once only, when accompanied by an adult, and during published opening times and arrangements. A charge may be made for special attractions which are not an integral part of the property itself.

The card can be used at any National Trust property with the exception of: Ashdown House, Bradley Manor, Hardwick Hall, and properties managed by English Heritage.

Voucher to be handed in.

This voucher is valid until end 1995.

....

NATIONAL TRUST FAMILY GROUP MEMBERSHIP COUPON
TO: **The National Trust, Membership Department, FREEPOST MB1438, Bromley, BR1 3BR**

Payment of £46 for your Family Group membership can be made by cheque or credit card. Cheques should be made payable to the National Trust, while credit card applications can be made direct on **0181 464 1111**. The lines are open Monday to Friday 9am to 5.30pm.

Please allow 28 days for receipt of your membership card. Subscription rate valid until 31 March 1996.

SOURCE CODE D136   DATE ....

FULL ADDRESS...

....

.... POSTCODE ....

TITLE   INITIALS   SURNAME   DATE OF BIRTH

....